I0831794

BLOOD OF THE DRAGON

WAYFINDER SERIES
BOOK 1

AMY ELIZABETH JOHNSON

KINDLE DIRECT PUBLISHING

Cover Design by Deffi Lesmawan

Hard Cover ISBN 979-8-9986351-0-6, 979-8-9986351-3-7

Paperback ISBN 979-8-9986351-1-3

eBook ISBN 979-8-9986351-2-0, 979-8-9986351-4-4

 Created with Vellum

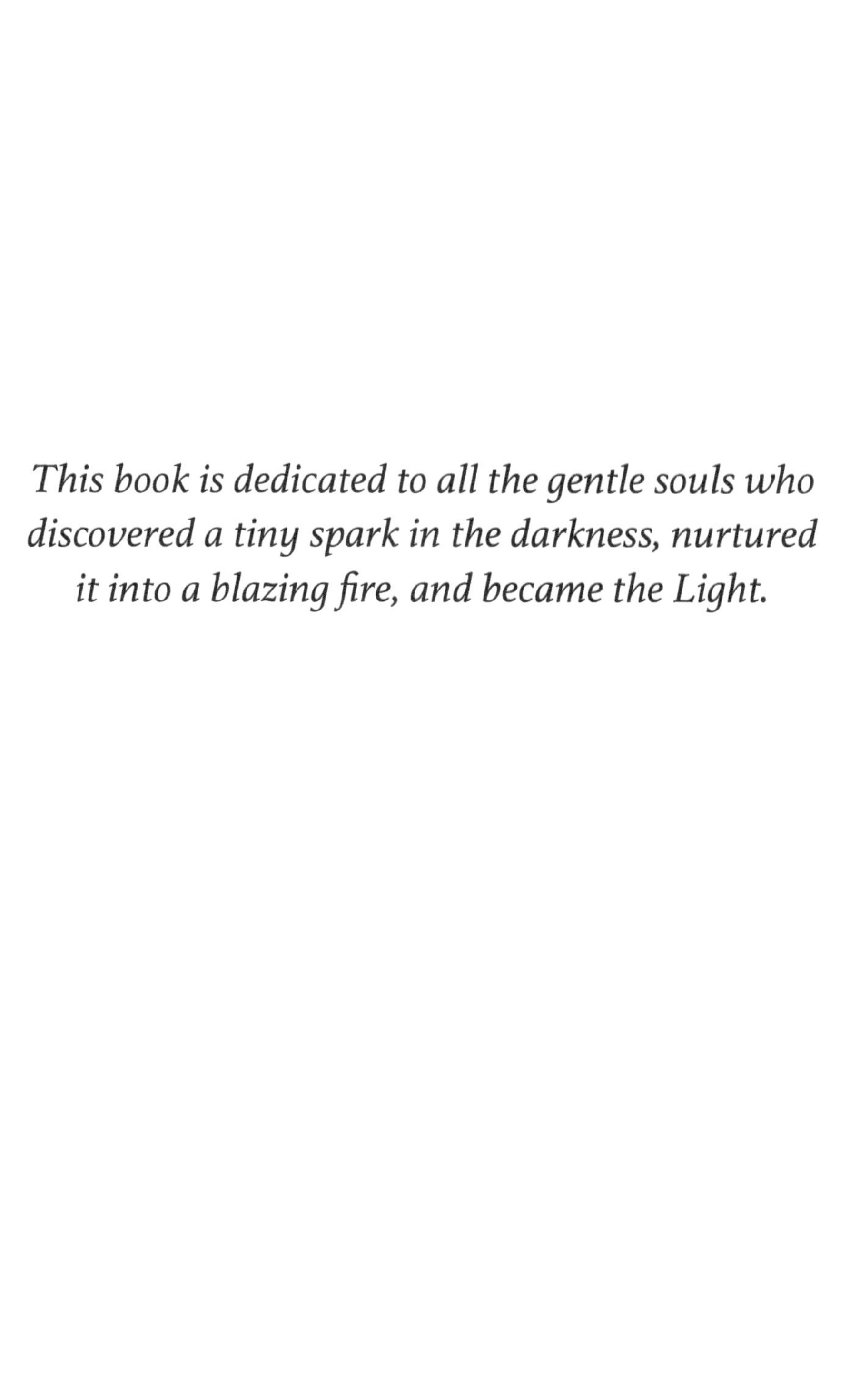

This book is dedicated to all the gentle souls who discovered a tiny spark in the darkness, nurtured it into a blazing fire, and became the Light.

CONTENTS

Part I : Embers & Scales 1
Chapter 1 3
Chapter 2 19
Chapter 3 25
Chapter 4 29
Chapter 5 37
Chapter 6 47
Chapter 7 53
Chapter 8 63
Chapter 9 79
Chapter 10 83
Chapter 11 97
Chapter 12 109
Chapter 13 123
Chapter 14 143
Chapter 15 153
Part II: The Mage 159
Chapter 16 161
Chapter 17 167
Chapter 18 175
Chapter 19 181
Part III: Beyond the Veil 189

Chapter 20 191
Chapter 21 207
Chapter 22 225
Chapter 23 235
Chapter 24 243
Chapter 25 251
Acknowledgments 261

About the Author 263

PART I : EMBERS & SCALES

Fire

Remember what you must do
When they undervalue you,
When they think
Your softness is your weakness,
When they treat your kindness
Like it is their advantage.
You awaken

Every dragon,
Every wolf,
Every monster
That sleeps inside you
And you remind them
What hell looks like when it wears the skin
Of a gentle human.

-Nikita Gill

CHAPTER 1

IO

I lean back against my favorite tree as I gaze up at the canopy. Yellow finches flit from branch to branch filling the air with bird song. Early morning sunlight filters through the oak leaves, golden light pools on the leaf strewn forest floor. I press my bare feet into the soft grass and breathe in the earthy scent of the forest.

"Io!," Mara calls through the trees.

If anyone else had come calling, I would have slunk deeper into the woods in search of a better hiding place. Princess Mara is my dearest friend. I am her hand maiden. My mother, Lady Brigid serves Queen Raya. House Greenwood took us in when my mother fled her homeland of Caelen. I never knew my father. I was only a babe when mother left.

Mara appears on the winding path, a warm smile illuminating her bright green eyes. Her auburn hair is in a plait, several stray wisps framing her lovely face. She wears an indigo gown which clings to her slight frame.

"I knew I'd find you here," Mara says as she settles down beside me, neatly crossing her legs beneath her deep blue skirts.

"Mistress Diedra was droning on about something or another," I say. "I just needed some air."

"Your absence was noted. She sent me to fetch you so that you can resume your lessons," Mara says as she plucks a white daisy from the grass.

"I was hoping to evade her for the rest of

the day. Is there anything you need of me, Your Grace?" I ask in my most reverent tone as I reach for my socks and boots.

"I ask only that you come quietly. My mother will strangle me if I soil my gown trying to drag you back to the castle," Mara says with a smirk.

"Well we can't have that now can we?" I say rising to my feet when I finish lacing my boots.

I extend my right hand to Mara and help her rise. We start down the path arm in arm. We grew up playing in these woods. The trees have heard every joyful laugh, caught every fallen tear, and held all of our secret dreams. It is our sanctuary. At the edge of our beloved forest the castle gardens take us into her arms. We wave to several staff who are gathering vegetables for the kitchens. Up ahead looms Greenwood Castle, the only home I have ever known. I take in the massive sandstone walls, spiraling towers, and ornate archways. Two guards nod in greeting as we approach the back entrance to the kitchens.

I breathe in the aroma of freshly baked bread as we step into the kitchens. I spot my mother tending to a large pot by the cook fire. She sprinkles rosemary and thyme into the simmering stew with her slender fingers. She turns at the sound of our footsteps, her deep brown eyes twinkling as she smiles at the pair of us. Her raven hair is swept up into a high bun. A smudge of flour on her left cheek lightens her tan complexion.

"Mistress Diedra was asking for you," my mother says handing us each a red apple from a near by basket.

"I'm on my way to see her," I sigh as I bite into my apple.

"Chin up, little bird. I'll have a bowl of venison stew ready when you finish your lesson," my mother says drawing me into her arms.

"I love you," I say returning her embrace. She smells of rosemary and fresh bread.

"I love you," she says releasing me. "I'll see you at supper."

Mara and I munch on our apples as we exit the kitchens. The stone corridor turns upward, leading us to the great hall above. We weave through the long empty tables to reach another corridor on the far side of the hall. We reach the large wooden doors of the castle library. I push them open. Mara follows me inside.

"Ah, Io at last," Mistress Diedra huffs as she rises from her chair by the hearth.

"My apologies, Mistress. I just needed some fresh air," I say bowing my head as I offer her a curtsey.

"Come my dear, let us pick up where we left off," Mistress Diedra says appeased. "Will you be joining us, Your Grace?"

"I suppose I could stay to keep an eye on this one," Mara says shooting me a wink.

We settle into the squashy armchairs surrounding the hearth. Mistress Diedra opens a book to begin our lesson. I stare into the flickering flames. Mistress Diedra is reading aloud from an ancient tome. Faded gold lettering on the cover reads, 'A History of Veridian.' Mara passes me some parchment and a quill. I watch as she scribbles notes furiously on her own parchment. I touch my own quill to my parchment as a deafening explosion outside rocks the castle. I clutch my quill in fear splattering my parchment with black ink. Screams and shouts reach our ears as we shoot to our feet. The library doors burst open and three royal guards sweep in.

"Princess Mara," gasps one I recognize as Sir Harald. "The castle is under attack. You must come with us. We'll get you all to safety."

Mara grabs my hand and pulls me toward the guards. Mistress Diedra scurries after us. My heart hammers in my chest as we race down the corridor. Sounds of clashing steel and battle cries reach us as we approach the great hall. The scene we take in is utter chaos. Greenwood soldiers are fighting enemy forces dressed in black. I am shocked to see that a number of the black warriors are *women*. Our freedom lies beyond a sea of green and black bodies. Swords clang, screams of agony tear at my ears, the granite floor is slick with blood, and the air reeks of death. A flash of silver catches my eye. I look to my left and lock eyes with a muscled warrior clad in black. He raises his sword over his head, bringing it down with such force the Greenwood knight he strikes crumples to the floor, never to rise again. His hazel eyes hold mine for only a heartbeat but, it feels like an eternity. He towers over the battlefield. His golden brown hair is tied in a knot atop his head. A long straight nose, high cheek bones, and a square jaw. Those smoldering hazel eyes.

Our royal guards draw us to the edge of the fray. We cower at their backs as they cut a path through the carnage. Countless limbs flail in every direction. The grunts of straining warriors intermingle with screams of agony and ragged last breaths. The smells of exertion and bloodshed invade our senses. I taste iron and salt on my tongue. We are jostled and shoved mercilessly. A muscular forearm catches me in the temple and I see stars. Mara's death grip on my arm is the only thing keeping me upright. I blink hard to focus my vision. By the grace of the Gods we make it across the hall unscathed. Sir Harald leads us back to the kitchens. A sob escapes me when I take in the bodies on the floor. I search frantically for my mother's form but, she is not among the dead. We slip out the door into the gardens. Thick black smoke is spilling from one of the towers. We run to the woods.

Sir Harald steers us off of the path into the cover of the trees. Branches tear at my dress and mark my bare forearms with angry red scratches. Sir Harald comes to an abrupt halt and I nearly crash into Mara.

"What have we here?," a menacing voice calls out.

I peer around the guards to see a tall, broad man dressed in black leather. His blonde hair is cropped short, his icy blue eyes bore into my soul, and his mouth is set in a wicked grin. My heart sinks when I realize he is not alone. Ten men of equal physique materialize from the surrounding forest, with swords drawn. Their leering eyes and snarling lips force me to take a step back. My blood runs cold.

"We are taking these women to safety," Sir Harald says firmly. "We are no threat to you."

"I'm afraid I can't let you do that," the man in black says. "I have specific orders to carry out."

"I didn't catch your name. What might these orders be?" Sir Harald says placing his right hand on his sword hilt. I see his knuckles whiten as he squeezes the blade's hilt. He shifts his feet into a fighting stance.

The man in black moves his hand to his own sword hilt. He curves his lips into a malevolent smile, his eyes hard as ice as he draws his blade.

"No need to trouble yourself with such details. It is a problem for another day. None of you will live to see tomorrow," the man in black sneers. He lunges at Sir Harald, wielding his sword with deadly precision. The two other royal guards in our company draw their swords to defend us. Sir Harald holds his own against the stranger in black, countering each strike with fervor. I clutch my skirts, poised to run. I tear my eyes away from Sir Harald and the man in black.

Mistress Diedra grabs Mara and I, pulling us behind a large blackberry bush before our enemies descend. My gut tells me we should run. My heart tells me we cannot abandon our brave knights. I have a simple hunting knife in my right boot. I have never used it on a person. Time seems to stand still. A sharp cry shatters my frantic thoughts. I peer through the blackberry brambles, Sir Harald has been wounded. My breath catches as I see him stumble. I am on my feet. The man in black kicks Sir Harald in the chest. Sir Harald crashes to the ground , his sword knocked from his hand. I rush forward as the man in black stalks over to Sir Harald as he struggles to stand. I am upon them before the stranger notices me. I swing Sir Harald's sword with everything I have, praying that it will be enough. The blade falls in downward arc, severing the man's outstretched sword arm. His eyes widen in shock as a primal scream tears from his lips. Blood spurts from the remaining stump of his left arm.

"You little bitch!" He screams in anguished rage as he rounds on me. He steps over Sir Harald and I nearly drop the sword as I stumble back.

The man in black snatches me by the throat lifting me from the forest floor. I kick and try to swing the sword. He tightens his hold. His eyes bore into mine. Panic consumes me as I struggle to pry his fingers loose. My vision blurs and the sword slips from my limp fingers. The world slips away as the darkness presses in on me. I am so tired. I just need to shut my eyes for a moment. My mind feels fuzzy. *What was I doing? I must have fallen asleep while Mistress Diedra was reading. I brace myself for her shrill voice.*

I try to lift my eyelids but, I cannot summon the strength. I slip further into the darkness. I am alone. I jump as a fire blazes to life on my left. The sound of the crackling flames echoes around me. The heat warms my skin. My feet move of their own accord. I approach the fire, mesmerized by the orange tongues that lick the shadows. I reach a tentative hand out. The hem of my dress catches fire and I shriek in fear. It takes mere seconds for my skirts to burn away. I realize that I can no longer feel the intense heat. I open my mouth to cry out but, there is no pain. *My blackened skin starts to form scales.* I gape at the shining obsidian scales that gleam in the fire light. My body tenses at the sound of a distant scream. I whirl around in search of danger. Suddenly I am falling through the darkness.

I am lying on the ground. My senses slowly return to me. Someone is writhing in pain next to me. I pry my eyelids open. The man in black is rolling along the ground clutching his right hand. It has been severely burned. I gag when I see the blistered remains of his right palm. My muscles are slow to respond when I attempt to silently crawl away from my attacker. I struggle to a sitting position and scan the clearing for Mara and Mistress Diedra. I stifle a sob when I see Mistress Diedra's still form. Her right arm is twisted at an odd angle. Her skirts have been hiked up around her hips, the bodice of her pale cream dress has been torn down the center. Stab wounds in her chest ooze crimson. Her blue eyes gaze upward at the sky she can no longer see. *May Nyx guide you safely home.*

Sir Harald and his fellow knights are lying still nearby. *Our valiant protectors, rest easy good Sirs.*

A scream reverberates through the trees. *Mara.* I shoot to my feet and take off in the direction of her screams. I crash through the underbrush as another scream rents the air. Mara is pinned to the forest floor by a brute with greasy black hair. Her indigo gown has been shredded. One meaty hand grips her hair while the other roams her body. I search the ground for a weapon. The best I can come up with is a jagged rock that I snatch in earnest. The man's back is to me so I slip up behind him and dash the rock against the back of his skull. It connects with a sickening crunch. The man collapses on top of Mara. I roll him off with difficulty and gather Mara into my arms. She is shaking violently, her breaths coming in ragged gasps, and her eyes staring blankly.

"Mara," I whisper gently. "It's me, Io. I've got you."

I reach down to take her hand in mine. My heart stops when I see the blood pouring from a deep wound in her chest. I press my hands to her wound. Mara's eyes are dimming, her skin is deathly cold to the touch. She blinks and meets my gaze. Tears shimmer in my eyes.

"Stay with me, Mara. I'm going to get you

some help. Just hang in there," I say as my voice cracks.

Mara squeezes my hand feebly. "You have to get out of here," Mara whispers. "Go now before they find you. Please, Io."

"I will not leave you here," I say stubbornly. "We'll go together."

"I will always be with you. Even if you can't see me," Mara smiles through her pain. One last act of love from my friend. The world will never be the same without her shining light.

"Mara," I gasp. Her chest rises and falls one last time as her eyelids flutter. Her face is so peaceful, she could be sleeping. I sit there numbly clutching the sister I loved. I lay her gently on the ground and cover her body with the remains of her dress. I stand on shaky legs and search for some flowers. A bed of primroses catches my eye. I pick several pristine blossoms. I place them on Mara's chest.

"Nyx, Goddess of Death, please guide my sister down the river. Keep her safe from harm," I pray. "I love you, Mara. Until we meet again."

My body feels heavy. My swollen throat throbs, each breath is burning agony. I clutch my right side. I think I may have broken a rib when I fell. The clouds cover the sun, plunging the temperature several degrees. I force my feet one in front of the other. I am unsure where to go. I wander through the trees, vaguely aware that I am headed towards the outer defenses at the edge of the woods. A large stone wall separates the castle grounds from the surrounding villages.

Black smoke is rising in the distance. A large hole has been blown through the towering stone wall up ahead. That must be how the warriors breeched the castle. I step through the smoldering remains of the wall. The closest village is just over the next hill. The eerie quiet does not lift my hopes of finding survivors.

CHAPTER 2

ROWAN

My footsteps echo throughout the great hall as I step over fallen bodies. Several Caelen warriors are emerging from the corridors with armfuls of all manner of jewelry and finery. I spot Bran among them and saunter over.

"There you are, Rowan," Bran says as he shoves a fistful of golden necklaces into a rucksack.

"Let's get out of here. Kade will want to be off before any aid can arrive," I say.

"I don't think that will be a problem," Bran

sighs. "We took them by surprise. No one made it out."

We join the others filing out of the great hall. We pass through the throne room and exit through the immense oak doors which have been thrown wide open. As we descend the steps, I take in the view of the surrounding countryside. A sea of green grass blankets rolling hills. The kingdom of Greenwood is nestled at the heart of an ancient forest. Its outer villages surround a pristine lake. I can see the Red mountains with their snowy peaks in the distance.

In the courtyard below, several captives are being loaded into wagons. A tall woman with a tan complexion and long black hair struggles against Ravana as she twists the woman's arm behind her back. The woman slams the back of her head into Ravana's nose. Ravana snarls and shoves the woman into the ground.

"You'll pay for that," Ravana whispers into

the woman's ear as she presses the side of her face into the dirt.

"Release me!" The woman spits back in our native tongue.

I meets Bran's gaze and raise a brow. Bran approaches Ravana.

"Get her on her feet," Bran orders. Ravana throws him a dirty look over her shoulder before she complies.

"What is your name?" I ask.

"Brigid, daughter of Eamon of House Flynn," the woman says straightening to her full height. "You will release me at once and find my daughter."

I turn to Ravana, "Bind her hands and bring her to Eamon's tent." Before Ravana can reply, I stride past. Bran falls into step beside me.

"Do you think she is who she claims to be?" Bran asks.

"We'll let the King be the judge of that," I say.

"What of her daughter?" Bran asks tossing his rucksack over his shoulder.

"She's probably among the dead," I say.

The sun hangs low on the horizon. Smoke clings to the earth and shrouds the land in a haze of grey. We pass warriors readying camp for the night. A large bonfire is being built, as well as pyres for the fallen. Greenwood and Caelen folk have been carried over the hills by the cartload. Several Caelen warriors have been tasked with setting the bodies on the pyres. King Eamon Flynn is among them.

"Glad to see you two are still among the living," King Eamon says by way of greeting.

"You as well," I return with a crooked smile.

"We just had a run in with a woman who claims to be your daughter," I say getting right to the point. Eamon detests small talk.

I study the King as he absorbs my words. He gently lays the body of a young Greenwood girl on her tiny pyre. When he straightens he meets my eyes with a stony expression.

"Bring her to me," Eamon says.

"I told Ravana to bring her to your tent," I say with a bow.

"Thank you, Rowan. I imagine Kade will be looking for you," Eamon says.

I give him a nod and take my leave with Bran. I have never met Eamon's daughter. Whispered stories around Caelen say that she ran off 18 years ago with her lover to escape an arranged marriage. As the daughter of the King, it was quite the scandal. Or so I am told, I was only two years old at the time. Brigid claimed to have a daughter but, mentioned no husband. I wonder if Eamon will lay his own granddaughter on a pyre tonight.

CHAPTER 3

IO

I rub the back of my hand against my eyes to dash away tears as I take in the remains of Briar village. The farmer's market has been cleaned out. Homes ransacked and burned to the ground. The bodies have been removed but, the blood stains lay bare the carnage that transpired here. These people were kind, hard working farmers. I doubt any had ever held a weapon in their lives.

I sift through the remains, hoping to find something useful. I enter a home that was spared from the fire. I open a chest at the end of a large bed. The contents have been rifled through. I pull out a dark green wool cloak. There are also several pairs of socks, clean linen shirts, and breeches. I peel off my tattered dress and remove my boots. I pull on the dark brown breeches and slip a linen shirt over my head. I pull my boots back on and drape the warm cloak around my shoulders. There is an empty rucksack on the floor. I find a few apples, carrots, and a hunk of bread under a wooden bowl on the table. I slip them into the rucksack and step outside. I turn back to the house and bow my head.

"Thank you," I whisper before turning away.

I walk through the town square. I pass the bakery where Mother and I would share a honey lemon cake on my birthday. The Seamstress's shop has been burned to the ground. I pray that Lila was able to make it out. She is my Mother's friend. The Apothecary still stands. I slip inside. Several shards of glass crunch under my boots. I find several useful elixirs and balms behind the counter. I add them to my pack along with several bundles of herbs, clean linen strips, and several knives. My Mother would visit Gaia often and I would play with her daughters and son while they discussed healing. The memories threaten to crush my resolve so I step back outside into the fading light.

Smoke continues to rise from the hill tops. The wind carries the smell of burning hair and flesh to me. *Funeral pyres. But whose*? I decide to creep closer. Maybe there are survivors I can join. I near the base of a hill and drop to my belly. I crawl up the hill and conceal myself in a scrubby bush next to an elm tree. There is a camp site below. I see no familiar faces. I spot a black banner with a golden dragon on it. I search my mind for a distant memory. Mistress Diedra always insisted we learn Veridian's noble houses. A golden dragon on a black field is the sigil of House Flynn. They rule the Kingdom of Caelen. My

Mother's homeland. *Maybe I have family down there. Family who just destroyed everything I have ever loved.*

I rest my head on my forearm as my head throbs. I gingerly feel my left temple and examine my bloody fingers. A wave of nausea sweeps over me as I try to stand, the ground tilts beneath my feet as my knees buckle. I fall hard on my back knocking the air from my lungs. I see the first evening star in the sky before I am plunged into darkness.

CHAPTER 4

ROWAN

The camp is quiet as I walk the perimeter on my watch. The bonfire still blazes bright to alert us to anyone approaching in the dead of night. I pass the last row of tents and climb a hill top to get a better view of camp. I lean against an elm tree and breathe in the crisp night air. The north winds have swept away the stench of death. I draw my cloak tighter around me to keep out the chill. A rustling sound at my feet has my dagger in my hand. I move around the elm tree and nearly step on a girl lying in the grass.

Her raven hair is fanned out around her face. Dark lashes brush rosy cheeks, her straight nose, and pink lips make for a beautiful countenance. Her light brown skin is smooth, full of youth and vitality. The left side of her face is smeared with dried blood. I kneel beside her and examine the deep purple bruises at her throat. I gently press my fingers to the base of her throat to check for a pulse. It is weak, fluttering like a bird's wings beneath my light touch. She is freezing. I gather her into my arms and rise.

As I start to descend the hill, her eyes open. She blinks as my face comes into focus. Her eyes are a warm brown like the earth after a summer rain. I feel her body tense as her eyes widen in panic. She squirms in my arms and I plant my feet to keep my balance.

"It's alright, I've got you. Lie still. You have a concussion," I say tightening my hold.

"Let me go," she protests pushing weakly against my chest.

I set her on her feet and she pitches forward immediately. I shoot my arm out to catch her before she falls on her face.

"I'm taking you to the healer. You are in bad shape. Can you tell me your name?" I ask.

"Io," she sighs as she collapses into my arms.

I lift her gently and continue down the hill. We have several healers with us. My Mother, Selene over sees them all. I move the tent flap aside and search for a place to lay Io. Helena, my Mother's apprentice rushes to help me.

"I found her up on the hill," I say.

"Poor dear, is frozen. Set her over here by the fire," Helena says leading me to an empty cot by the brazier.

I place Io on the cot and turn to leave. Helena retrieves a bowl and linen cloth. She pours hot water from a kettle into the bowl. I glance over my shoulder before I step out. Helena tenderly wipes the dried blood from Io's face. I step back out into the cold.

The first rays of sunlight peak over the Red Mountains. I join King Eamon by the dying bonfire.

"Your Grace," I say bowing my head.

"Commander," King Eamon replies meeting my eyes. His green eyes have dark shadows beneath them. I suspect he has been pacing through the night.

"The castle has been emptied. The dead have been put to rest. The royal family, with the exception of Princess Mara, have been detained. We found the Princess's body in the woods. It seems one of our own did not recognize her. She was raped and stabbed," I report flatly.

"I will see that man put to death," King Eamon says through gritted teeth.

"No need, Your Grace," I say. "We found his body near the Princess. His skull was smashed in with a rock."

"Very well. On to the next matter at hand,"

King Eamon says wearily. "I will designate warriors to carry out the restoration of Greenwood castle and the surrounding villages. I will be leaving my son, Killian behind to over see the construction. You and the remaining forces will accompany me back to Caelen."

"Yes, Your Grace," I say with a bow.

"I'd like to properly introduce you to my daughter, Brigid," King Eamon says raising a bushy black eyebrow. "The girl you found on the hilltop this morning is my granddaughter."

"It is a blessing to be reunited with your family after all this time, Your Grace," I say.

"A blessing indeed," King Eamon murmurs as he gazes into the fire, his expression unreadable.

"I will begin the breakdown of camp, Your Grace," I say with a bow.

"Thank you, Rowan," King Eamon says gazing into the embers.

I leave the King to his thoughts and make my way to the cook tent. Finn is serving porridge and eggs. I grab a wooden bowl and stand in line. Bran falls in behind me with a bowl of his own.

"Morning, Sunshine," Bran yawns as he stretches his arms over head.

"Morning," I say taking in his unruly black curls and tired blue eyes.

Bran and I are of a height. His skin is fair and he is well muscled from years of fighting for our good King Eamon. We have been friends since we were stick fighting boys with big dreams. Our Mothers are sisters. My Aunt Gwen works alongside my Mother healing the sick and wounded.

"Picked up a girl last night, did you?" Bran says nudging me with his bowl.

"She was unconscious for the brief time we spent together," I say rolling my eyes.

"Well perhaps she will thank you properly for saving her life," Bran says with a mischievous grin.

"I did not wait around for her to wake. She won't even remember me," I say dismissively.

"Strapping fellow like you?" Bran persists. "She'll remember."

I give my friend a small smile. Bran is always looking for a woman to warm his bed. He has no problem finding an eager lass. He is always trying to make me a match. No one has ever peeked my interest. I think of Io beneath the elm tree with her raven hair, rosy cheeks, and soft lips. Those brown eyes.

The line lurches forward and we collect our breakfast. Bran and I find a log near the newly rekindled fire. The heat eases my sore muscles. I stretch my legs out in front of me and taste my porridge. My eyes sweep over camp and I spot a green cloak in the crowd. *Io.* She looks steady on her feet today. I can see five neat stitches along her left temple, Helena's work. Bran follows my line of sight and lets out a low whistle.

"You sure know how to pick 'em," Bran smirks. "Go talk to her."

"I don't have anything to say," I mumble around a mouthful of eggs.

“How about, ‘how are you feeling?’ Bran suggests. ‘Let me properly introduce myself, Rowan McGlaughlin of Caelen.’

Bran hauls me to my feet and pushes me in the direction of the breakfast line. I hand him my wooden bowl and take a deep breath as I walk towards my fair maiden.

CHAPTER 5

IO

I wake in the grey dawn light. My surroundings slowly come into focus. I sit bolt upright when I realize I am in a tent. I groan loudly as my head pounds and my stomach roils.

"Easy now, lass," a kind voice says to my right. I turn to see an older woman in a red dress. Her blonde hair is braided and pinned neatly atop her head. She has warm hazel eyes and a bright smile. I feel my own lips curving into a smile.

"Thank you for caring for me," I say

hoarsely. I clear my throat and try my voice again, "I am Io."

"Good to meet you, Io. I am Selene, my son, Rowan found you on the hilltop and brought you to camp," Selene explains.

The warrior from the great hall. I thought I was dreaming. He took me into his arms.

"I am most grateful for your kindness," I say, hoping the Selene did not notice me blush.

"You have a visitor," Selene says. My Mother rises from a chair in the corner that I did not notice until now. My eyes sting with tears as she gently hugs me.

"Mistress Diedra and Mara are dead," I say numbly.

"I know," my Mother says, her voice thick with unshed tears. "I helped light the pyres."

I free my legs from the tangle of blankets. Selene offers me a steaming mug of tea. I clutch the mug to my chest and breathe in the steam. Mother helps me to my feet. Selene leads me to a tub so that I can wash. I strip and ease into the warm water. Selene and my Mother slip away to give me some privacy. They settle down at a table to finish their tea.

The gray dawn light filtering through the tent entrance gradually brightens. I listen to the camp coming back to life. The smell of breakfast cooking makes my stomach growl. Selene lays a fresh set of clothes on the chair next to the tub.

"Finn should have breakfast ready soon," Selene says with a smile. "Do you feel up to stretching your legs?"

"Yes, I can manage," I say accepting the towel that Selene offers.

I dry and dress quickly in the cool morning air. Selene has gifted me a grey pair of pants, a deep blue tunic, and some black wool socks. I find my boots next to the cot and pull them on.

"Thank you for the clothes," I say.

"Of course, dear heart," Selene replies. "When you leave the tent, take a left, the cook tent is at the end of our row."

I leave my Mother and Selene to their conversation. I still feel unsteady on my feet but, I do not want them to fuss over me. I take in the camp site as I walk down the row of tents. Soldiers dressed in all black emerge from their tents to receive their orders for the day. A group of female warriors are breaking down tents and loading them into a wagon. A tall fair woman with blonde hair catches my eye. She glares at me and flicks her hair over her shoulder as she turns away. *Look at me, making friends already*.

A line of people has formed outside the cook tent. I stand behind a short man with greasy black hair. His pungent smell forces me back a step. A dull ache in my skull makes my eyelids heavy. I contemplate making my way back to the healer's tent.

"You don't look so good," a deep voice says.

I turn to see the warrior from the great hall regarding me with a furrowed brow. He reaches an arm out to steady me.

"I'm fine," I say. He lowers his arm but, looks unconvinced.

"You're Selene's son?" I ask.

"Yes, I'm Rowan," he says.

"Thank you for helping me, Rowan," I say. "I'm Io."

"You're welcome," Rowan says. "Do you want to go back to the tent? You look like you need to lie down."

"I can manage," I say stubbornly as I sway slightly on my feet.

"I can see that," Rowan says with a smirk. "I'll just stand right here, should you need me."

"As you wish," I say praying the relief I feel does not show on my face.

The line moves fairly quickly. A man with a black curls and a beard greets us at the front of the line.

"Good morning," the cook says offering me a steaming bowl.

"Good morning," I return accepting the bowl. "Thank you."

I step away from the cook, unsure where to go. Rowan takes me by the elbow and steers me to a log by the fire. Most people have finished their breakfast and are heading off to help with the breakdown of camp. I sit down and eye Rowan warily.

"Where's your food?" I ask seeing his empty hands.

"I ate earlier," Rowan says.

"I'm fine really," I say. "You don't need to stay with me."

"Trying to get rid of me?" Rowan asks.

"I'm just saying if you need to be somewhere, don't let me keep you," I say growing annoyed with the conversation.

"No where else I need to be at the moment," Rowan says meeting my eyes.

My cheeks feel hot. I feel like he is peering into my very soul. I look away, desperate for a distraction. Right on cue, a young boy carrying an armful of potatoes trips in front of us. He lands in a heap at Rowan's feet, potatoes scattering everywhere. Rowan gently lifts the boy to his feet. I set my bowl down and gather up the potatoes. The boy flashes us a shy smile before he scurries away toward the cook tent.

"Shall I walk you back to the Healers?" Rowan asks. "Or can you manage?"

That earns him a smile from me. "I suppose company would be nice," I say.

I gather up my untouched porridge bowl and fall into step beside Rowan. I study his profile. His golden brown hair is gathered in a neat knot. Golden lashes fan out above his hazel eyes flecked with gold. His nose is long and straight, flanked by high cheek bones. He has a pleasant mouth filled with straight white teeth and a strong jaw. *Absolutely gorgeous. Most likely nothing but trouble.* I blush when he catches me staring. *I need to get away from this man.*

"Your mother is from Caelen," Rowan says. "I know your grandfather."

"I have never met him," I say. "Is he a good man?"

"He is a good King," Rowan says. "He takes care of our people. I will let you decide if he is a good man."

"Do good men destroy homes and put innocent people to the sword?" I ask, not bothering to soften the edge in my voice.

"Good men are capable of terrible things when they think their cause is just," Rowan says.

"And what cause would that be?" I ask.

"Elaria has been killing our kind for generations," Rowan says with an edge of his own.

"Your kind?" I say in confusion.

"Mages, shape shifters, any magic folk they can get their hands on," Rowan says with disgust.

"Magic?" I say puzzled. "Are you saying my Mother has magic?"

"Of course," Rowan says puzzled by my confusion. "You are a daughter of Caelen."

"Sorry to disappoint, I have no magic," I say dismissively.

"You have never tried to awaken it. Our people can show you how to control your power," Rowan says.

We have reached the Healers's tent. Rowan turns to face me. I tense at his proximity. My head is swirling with questions. My stomach twists at the thought of my mother hiding her past from me.

"Give us a chance," Rowan says. "You might like what you find."

"Us?" I ask raising my brows.

"Meaning the people of Caelen," Rowan clarifies. "I'm not opposed to your idea of *us* though," Caelen says with a wink.

My heart pounds and I feel dizzy again. *Ugh, what is wrong with me? He probably says that to every woman he sees. Get a hold of yourself.*

"I'm sure you have plenty of interested women to help you in that regard," I say rolling my eyes.

"None that have ever caught my eye," Rowan says simply.

"And what of your heart?" I venture.

A smile tugs the corner of his lips. "None that have captured my heart either," Rowan says.

He raises my right hand to his lips and gently presses a kiss to the back of my hand. His kiss floods my body with warmth, a lingering spark dances along my skin. Rowan gives me another wink. He turns and departs without another word. *I'm doomed.*

CHAPTER 6

IO

We have been riding for hours. I stand up in the stirrups so I can stretch my legs. I stifle a yawn as my horse side steps a broken branch over hanging the path. My eyes find Rowan riding ahead. He sits tall atop his mount and my eyes linger on his broad back as he makes his way through the trees. I feel a whoosh of air as something streaks past my face. The tree to my left has an arrow has sunk deep into the bark. A trail of amber sap oozes from the wound in the bark. My heart thunders in my ears as I throw myself from the saddle. My ankle catches on a tree root and I crash to the ground.

I struggle to fill my lungs with air as I scramble to my feet. I whirl around to look for the other women. Bandits have materialized from the forest. I feel the blood drain from my face as a burly man with pale skin and red hair seizes one of the washer women by her throat. I run towards them, determined to help. My feet are ripped out from under me as a large arm grips my waist. A scream tears out of my chest as a filthy hand gropes my breast. Sour ale breath invades my nose.

"I do love a good scream," a gravely male voice rasps in my ear.

I thrash and kick. The man presses cool steel to my throat.

"Be a good girl," he slurs. I freeze and search desperately for help.

The wagons are on fire. Two women lay dead in the grass. Their dresses torn down the front, exposing their breasts. Blood pools beneath their still forms. I whimper in despair as hot tears sting my eyes. The man grips my shoulder and roughly spins me around to face him. He looms over me, a wall of muscle. He leers at me with black eyes. His thin lips curl into a wicked smile. In one swift motion he draws a knife and slashes down the front of my shirt. I flinch away as his knife slices my breastbone. A massive hand shoots out at me. He seizes a fistful of my hair, yanking my head back. I let out another scream. He silences me with a punch to the gut.

I fall to my knees, gasping for air. Spots dance across my vision. He places the toe of his boot against my left shoulder and kicks viciously. I strike the back of my head on the grass. I gaze up at the sky in a daze. I hear the tearing of fabric. I can feel cool air on my thighs. My eyelids droop and my mind is foggy. I feel a sharp pain deep inside me and my eyes fly open. The man has me pinned beneath him, his trousers around his ankles. I beat my hands against his back weakly. I scream in rage as he invades me. He backhands me across the face and I taste blood.

My breathing is ragged, my pulse racing. I can feel heat building beneath my skin. *Why is it so hot? I am burning up.* I squirm and manage to free my right arm. I claw his face and kick my legs wildly. I shove his face away from me as I try to unseat him.

A shrill scream rings out and I smell sizzling flesh. My mouth falls open as I stare at my right hand pressed against my attackers face. The skin beneath my hands has erupted in angry red welts. His eyes are wide with horror. He howls and claws at my hands. *I am burning him with my touch.*

I gag as I take in the melted remains of the left side of his face. *What is happening?* The man falls backward, writhing in pain on the ground. I stare in utter shock. I shake my head and force myself to move. I lunge at his writhing form. I take a hold of his weapon and squeeze with all my might. An anguished cry rips out of his scorched lips. The blistered skin cracks and bleeds. I release his vile member and stomp down viciously with my boot before I take off. He reaches down to his crotch and screams in a blind rage.

His screams follow me as I crash through the trees. They will haunt my dreams for the rest of my life. Sharp branches tear at my clothes as I run with reckless abandon. I cast a backward glance over my shoulder and crash into a broad chest. I land hard on my back and lie still. Pain washes over me, pulling me down into its dark depths. The last thing I see is a hand brushing the hair from my face.

CHAPTER 7
ROWAN

I scan the tree line as we make our way through the dark forest that divides Elaria and Caelen. All Veridian children are warned to never stray too close to Fae Forest. *Sorcha, Daughter of the Forest* walks among the trees, protector of maidens, animals, and the earth. Honor her forest and pass unharmed as a friend. Enter with malevolent intent and suffer her wrath.

"Oi! Are you listening to me?" Bran calls over, shaking me from my thoughts. "Dreaming of your girl?"

"Not my girl," I say. *Not yet. I'm not giving up that easily.*

"Well if you want to change that, you better hurry before the King marries her off," Bran says with a pointed look.

I sigh. *He has a point.* "What do you propose I do to win the heart of the fair maiden?"

"Teach her to fight," Bran says as though it is the most obvious choice.

"What?" I ask, gaping at him.

"Teach her to fight," Bran repeats as if I am slow in the head. "A useful skill to learn and it gives you an excuse to get close to her."

I tilt my head to the side considering. "That might not be a bad idea," I admit.

"All of my ideas are good ideas," Bran says taking a bite out of a dried beef strip.

I snort. "Sure they are," I say.

I have not seen Io since I walked her back to the Healer's tent. I am riding at the front of our caravan. The Healer's travel in the middle of the caravan alongside the King. We will ride until dusk and then make camp inside the Caelen boundary.

A scream from behind has Bran and I whipping our horses around. Shouts rise up and three short blasts from a hunting horn announce an attack. I urge my mare forward. Bran follows close behind. I dig my heels into Nyx's sides as another long scream pierces the air. Thick black smoke rises into the sky. The wagons are ablaze. Dark green clad figures are dragging the Healers away from the wagons by their hair. I draw my sword and charge at the nearest enemy. He turns just as I am upon him, eyes wide in shock. I bring my sword down and sever his head before he can scream. His brown eyes are wide, his mouth slack as his severed head tumbles to the ground. His body crumples to the forest floor. The woman he was dragging scrambles to her feet and takes off running.

I find my Mother on the other side of the fray, hiding behind an ash tree with Helena and Brigid. I cut down every bandit in my path to get to them. Blood splatters my face as I yank my sword from the belly of a fat bandit with an eye patch. My mother's frantic eyes land on me and she gives me a nod to let me know she is unharmed.

Two Healers lay dead in the grass, rivulets of blood staining the ground crimson. Bran and the Royal Guard have secured the King and the other Healers. A flash of dark green draws my gaze. A figure in a dark green cloak sprints through the trees.

A howl echoes through the forest, setting my nerves on edge. I realize that I know this frantic individual. Her expression is one of pure terror. *Gods, she's fast.* I move to intercept her. She glances over her shoulder and collides with me. I stagger back a step as Io is flung backward. I crouch down and brush the hair from her face. Her brow is sleek with sweat and her eyes are unfocused, her eyelids flutter closed.

My heart shatters at the sight of her. Her shirt has been sliced. A shallow cut down her breastbone. Her right eye has started to blacken. I clench my hands into fists when I see the stain of blood on the inside of her pants leg. I vow to flay the man who laid his hands her.

I gently gather Io into my arms. The back of her head is bleeding profusely. Her golden brown skin has gone deathly pale. I swallow a lump in my throat as I walk back towards the others. My Mother and Helena rush over when they see us.

"I'll tend to her, my son," my Mother says gently placing her hands on my shoulder.

"She was raped," I say hollowly. "Her injuries are extensive. She hit the back of her head."

"I will brew a tea to prevent a babe," my Mother says gazing upon Io's face. "We will heal her body. Time and love will heal her soul."

I carry Io to the remaining wagon. I set her down on a pile of furs. My Mother climbs inside and gets to work. I watch as she turns Io on her side to check the back of her head. She lovingly wipes blood away with a damp cloth.

"How is she?" Bran asks as he comes to stand beside me.

"She's in good hands," I say.

"King Eamon wants to continue onto Cae-len," Bran says. "You should stay close to Io. I can take the lead."

I nod my thanks. Bran pats my back as he takes his leave. Nyx is grazing near by. I lead her over to the Healers. Helena and Selene are covering the dead with white sheets.

"I'll bring wood for a pyre," I offer.

"Thank you, Rowan," Helena says in a quavering voice.

"I'll help you," Brigid says rising to her feet.

Brigid follows me into the trees. I gather broken branches to construct a pyre. I watch Brigid gather sticks and tinder. The sun is obscured by grey clouds. An autumn breeze stirs the leaves of red and gold that cover the forest floor. The leaves swirl up into the air, dancing with the wind.

"Why didn't you tell her about Caelen?" I ask without preamble.

Brigid looks up from her armful of kindling. "I was trying to protect her," Brigid says tightly. "Elaria is not safe for our kind."

"She deserves the truth," I say, over stepping my bounds.

"And she will have it," Brigid snaps, her eyes ablaze.

Brigid turns on her heel and makes her way back to camp. I snatch a few more fallen tree limbs and follow Brigid. I busy myself with building the pyre. My Mother managed to salvage some herbs, balms, and tinctures from one of the wagons. She murmurs to herself as she surveys her inventory. I place the last tree branch on the pyre. I lift the first body and place it on the pyre. I place the second body beside it.

King Eamon approaches. His brows are

drawn together and he looks older somehow as though the last few hours have taken a toll.

"We're ready to move out," King Eamon says. "Let's make haste to Caelen before nightfall."

"Yes, Your Grace," I say bowing.

King Eamon sighs heavily. "Thank you for seeing to my granddaughter," he says gruffly.

"I should have been there sooner," I say gripping the hilt of my sword.

King Eamon fixes me with his green eyes and offers me a half smile. "Do not be hard on yourself, son. We cannot spare the ones we love from all the ugliness of this world. What we can do is walk beside them in the darkness and help them find their way back to the light."

We ride in silence through the thinning trees at the edge of the forest. We reach Caelen as the sun is sinking below the horizon. The north winds sweep across the grasslands carrying the salty scent of the sea beyond. We head for a grove of pine trees near the sea cliffs.

The warriors at the head of our party have already begun setting up camp when the Healers and I arrive. I dismount and lead Nyx over to a towering pine tree. I remove her saddle and she nudges my hand with her nose to show her gratitude.

The horses pulling the wagon snort as we relieve them of their burden. I walk around to the back of the wagon to check on Io. I am surprised to find her awake.

"You should be resting," I scold.

The corner of Io's mouth twitches and a flicker of light shines from her eyes. She struggles to sit up. I help her into a sitting position. The effort has drained all the color from her face. I keep my hand on her back to steady her.

"I don't want to sleep," Io says softly.

"Would you like some company?" I ask.

"Sure," Io says patting the floor of the wagon beside her.

I settle down next to her, careful not to touch her. Everyone has begun to set up camp. *I should get a tent set up for Io. She is unwell.*

"I am going to find a place for you to lie down and rest," I say. "Stay here, I'll come back and get you."

Io nods. I help her lay back down. I rush off to ready a tent.

CHAPTER 8

IO

The sound of crashing waves reaches my ears. I gasp as I take in the golden sun sinking into the sea. The sky is a swirl of orange, pink, and gold. The waves crashing upon the rocks at the base of the cliff spray sea foam into the air. I watch the water slip off of the smooth stones and return to the churning sea.

Rowan left to help finish camp set up. He told me to rest but, I cannot resist getting my first good look at the sea. I wince as I drag myself over to the edge of the wagon and gingerly lower myself to the grass. I slowly wander over to the cliffs. My head throbs with each step. I breathe in the sea air and close my eyes.

"Everyone pulls their weight around here," a derisive voice says behind me. I don't bother to turn around.

I hear boots stomping through the grass. A hand grips my left shoulder and spins me around. I stand face to face with the blonde warrior who glared at me back at camp in Elaria. Her long thin face is set in a snarl, her icy blue eyes staring daggers at me. I have no clue what I have done to illicit such a response. I stare back at her and hold my ground.

"What's the matter? Your first tumble not what you expected?" She taunts. "I'm sure one of the men will bed you again." Her friends snicker and look down their noses at me.

My breath catches and I fight to keep my expression neutral. My skin crawls as I smell his sour ale breath. I feel his calloused hands pawing at my breasts, kicking me to the ground, and forcing my legs apart. I curl my hands into fists and launch myself at the bitch. I relish the look of shock and pain in her wide blue eyes as I slam her to the ground. Someone is screaming as I slam my fists into her face. Blood spurts from her nose and she sputters, struggling to unseat me. I am no fierce warrior but, I am strong from working at the castle all my life. I trap her torso between my knees, pinning her arms against her sides as I unleash my rage. Her right eye is beginning to swell shut. Strong arms hook under mine and haul me backward. The blonde tries to rise, I aim a vicious kick at her. She lets out a grunt as it connects with her jaw. Someone is still screaming. I thrash against the arms holding me tight.

"Io! It's me," Rowan pants.

I slowly still and Rowan releases me. My throat burns and my voice is hoarse. The screams were *mine*. The two women who accompany the blonde are trying to rouse her.

The one with red hair shoots me a dirty look over her shoulder. I blow her a kiss.

"I see you can manage after all," Rowan says struggling to keep the amusement from his voice.

I huff out a half hearted laugh. My body is shaking. Rowan reaches a hand out to steady me.

"It's just the adrenaline," Rowan says in a low voice. "You'll be alright once your blood cools."

I fear I might vomit so I simply nod. A middle aged man with short cropped blonde hair strides over with clenched fists.

"TERRA!" the blonde man shouts. He rounds on me and Rowan steps forward to shield me.

"Get out of my way, Rowan," the man seethes. "That little cunt attacked my daughter!"

"Your daughter and her friends were the aggressors," Rowan says with menace.

"I will not stand for this," the red faced

man booms. "I am the Lord Commander. I demand this wretch be punished!"

"What's all this?" King Eamon says arriving on the scene with a deep frown.

"Your Grace," Lord Commander bows to the King. "This girl attacked my daughter!"

"Were there any witnesses, Kade?" King Eamon asks evenly as he fixes the Lord Commander with a withering stare.

"Your Grace," Rowan says bowing to the King. "I saw the exchange. Sara provoked Io. Io acted in self defense."

Lord Commander Kade levels me with a venomous glare. I hold his grey gaze. *You don't scare me, prick. I'll beat the evil right out of her.*

"This *girl* is my flesh and blood," King Eamon says coldly. "Tell your *daughter* to keep her forked tongue behind her teeth if she wants to keep her head."

"Yes, Your Grace," Lord Commander Kade says through gritted teeth. He bows stiffly and stalks off to collect his daughter.

King Eamon turns to me. I swallow and

ready myself for the reprimand. He meets my gaze with tired green eyes and his lips curve up in a smile. I glance at Rowan in alarm. Rowan suppresses a smile of his own.

"You're your mother's daughter," King Eamon says with a chuckle. The corner of his eyes crinkle and a dimple appears on his left cheek.

A shaky laugh escapes my lips. I see my mother in his face. His short black hair has some streaks of grey. The lines on his forehead and either side of his wide mouth tell of the toll ruling has taken. He must be sixty years old but, his body is strong. I do not doubt his ability to swing the sword at his hip.

"Come, let us join your mother for supper," King Eamon says. "Will you join us, Rowan?"

"As you wish, Your Grace," Rowan says inclining his head.

We turn away from the cliff and walk toward the pine trees. The pounding of my heart gradually subsides. I glance at Rowan who gives me a reassuring smile. Camp has been set up among the pine trees. A bonfire blazes in the center. Raucous laughter rises from the warriors taking their supper around the fire. I see two lovers entwined, sharing a kiss. I look away to allow them their privacy. In my eighteen years of life, I have never been kissed. I had never lain with a man. I dreamt of falling in love. Giving myself to the man I love, body and soul. I look up at Rowan beside me as he covers the ground with his long strides. My eyes settle on his lips and I turn my eyes downward to hide my blush.

King Eamon leads us to his personal tent. We enter and find my mother and Selene waiting for us. My mother looks down to my bloody knuckles but, makes no comment. Rowan and King Eamon make no mention of my run in with Terra. I take a seat next to my mother at a long oak table. Rowan and Selene sit opposite us. King Eamon settles at the head of the table. The spread before us looks delectable. A golden brown turkey surrounded by roasted pumpkin, peppers, potatoes, and carrots; a large loaf of honey rosemary bread with creamy butter; a bowl of blueberries; luscious red apples; and a pumpkin pie with whipped cream.

"Please eat," King Eamon says helping himself to some turkey and vegetables.

I did not realize how hungry I was. I fill my plate and take a bite of turkey. It is tender and moist. I taste salt, pepper, garlic, rosemary, sage, and thyme. I suspect the cook conjured this food with magic. *How else could he prepare such a fine meal out here*?

"Allow me to address the elephant in the room," King Eamon says clearing his throat. We all turn to him in unison, waiting expectantly.

"As you have no doubt heard from the camp gossips, Io, you are my granddaughter and heir to the throne of Caelen," King Eamon says simply. *As if he had not just up ended my life for the second time this week.*

"Father, perhaps we can discuss this another time…" My mother starts.

"I think you've kept the truth from her long enough, Brigid," Grandfather cuts in sharply. I flinch at his sharp tone. "Io has a right to know her origins. She deserves to know the family you kept from her." I raise my eyes to him when I hear the emotion in his voice.

"And she will," my mother says angrily. "She is my daughter and I did what I had to do to protect her."

Selene clears her throat. "Your Grace," Selene says gently. "Perhaps my son and I should take our leave?"

"My apologies, Selene," Grandfather says softening. "My daughter and I have much to discuss. Please return to your supper. We will take our discussion outside."

"Forgive me, Selene. Rowan," my mother says setting her napkin down as she rises from her seat. "I'll return shortly, Io," she says, giving me a small smile. Before I can protest, they exit the tent, leaving me alone with Selene and Rowan.

"This turkey is divine," Rowan says around a mouthful.

Selene scowls and aims a kick at his shin which Rowan dodges easily. I burst out laughing. Selene swats Rowan's arm and he smiles at her with such love. Rowan catches me watching him. I lower my eyes to the table. He gently takes my hand in his. I look up. Rowan gives my hand a gentle squeeze. Warmth floods my skin, the pain from my throbbing knuckles ebbs. I give him a quizzical look. Rowan simply winks and releases my hand. I gasp as I examine my hand. The skin of my knuckles is smooth and unbroken once more. The dried blood smeared across the back of my hand the only evidence of my injury.

"Healing is your magic?" I ask.

"Among other things," Rowan says raising his palm. I feel the heat before his palm erupts in blue flames. The flames lick at his fingers. A small ball of dancing blue flame hovers above his upturned palm.

"I am an Elemental," Rowan says flicking his wrist. The blue flames extinguish, leaving a pale blue curls of smoke in their absence. "I can produce and manipulate fire. I can also heal myself and others."

"That is a useful gift," I say awestruck as I absorb this new magical information.

"Does my mother have a magic?" I ask.

Rowan looks to Selene. She hesitates and lets out a sigh. I hold my breath as I silently plead for an answer to one of many questions burning in my chest.

"Your mother is an Earth Elemental," Selene says. "Brigid can control the forces of nature- the trees, plants, rocks, the very ground beneath our feet."

"Who was my father?" I press.

"His name was Connor," Selene says sadly. "He was a Water Elemental. He could manipulate water. When he saw your mother, she bewitched him, body and soul. There was no truer love."

Selene clasps my hand. "You are a product of true love," she says with a smile. "You have your mother's wisdom and beauty. Your father's brave heart and warrior spirit."

I blink away tears and nod slowly. My voice fails me. I cannot ask my next question. Selene spares me, giving the answer freely.

"Your mother was betrothed to Lord Commander Kade. When she fell in love with your Father, they decided to run. Kade is a cruel man. She left to live a life of her choosing. Your Grandfather was heartbroken."

"Why did Caelen attack Elaria?" I ask, eager for more answers.

"The Elaria you think you know is very different from the Elaria we know," Selene says. "Caelen is home to all sorts of Magic. Elaria has envied our gifts for centuries. Past Kings and Queens of Elaria have captured and enslaved Caelen people. Elaria uses their magic to serve their own ends."

"I have never heard that story," I say sadly. *I feel as if my whole life has been a lie.*

"I'm sure you haven't heard many stories, dear heart," Selene says gently.

"Thank you for telling me," I say.

"I'll go check on your Mother," Selene says rising from her chair. "You two enjoy."

My head is reeling. I don't think I can take any more stories tonight. Rowan seems to sense my unease.

"How about a walk?" Rowan says turning toward me.

"Sure," I say absently.

I tidy my plate and push my chair in. Rowan holds the tent flap aside for me. I take a deep breath of the night air. I shiver and pull my cloak around me. Rowan walks at my side. A smattering of stars twinkles in the black sky. A half moon lights our path as we wind our way through the tents. The bonfire is still blazing at the heart of camp. Two men sit opposite each other by the fire, playing a game of cards.

Rowan does not try to strike up a conversation. I am grateful for his intuition. We walk in comfortable silence. It feels as though I have known him my whole life. The fact that we met a mere three weeks ago, seems absurd. He makes me feel *safe*. I don't feel like I have to put on a smile for Rowan. Being with him is as familiar as breathing. I am both unsettled and curious about this feeling.

"I can hear you thinking from here," Rowan jests.

"I hope not," I say with a laugh.

"That bad, huh?" Rowan asks with a crooked smile.

I lose myself in those hazel eyes. I trip over a fallen pine branch. Rowan shoots his arm out to steady me. His hands hold me fast but, his grip is gentle. I swallow as I study his strong forearms and biceps. My eyes drag over his muscled chest and settle on his mouth, lips slightly parted.

"You're rather clumsy," Rowan says with mock annoyance.

"You just make me weak in the knees," I fire back.

We dissolve into a fit of laughter. I feel tears at the corners of my eyes, a weight lifting off my chest. Rowan pulls me to his chest and I still, my breath catching. Rowan eases me away and lowers his arms to his sides. I take a deep breath. I search his eyes as I close the distance between us. I can see gold flecks in his eyes. I turn my face up to his and we share a single breath.

"We should get back," Rowan says.

"Right," I say blinking.

I start to turn away. Rowan wraps an arm around my waist, pulling me flush with him and then his mouth is on mine. Warmth spreads across my lips as I taste his fire. Rowan weaves his fingers into my hair. I press my hips into him and arch my back as he trails a hand down my spine. *I am bewitched, body and soul.*

CHAPTER 9

ROWAN

Io's luminous brown eyes sparkle as she tilts her head back and laughs. It is the most beautiful sound, full of joy and warmth. I decide to make her laugh more often. I pull her to my chest and she freezes. My heart twists as I see fear flicker behind her eyes. I create some space between us to ease her mind.

"We should get back," I say breathing in her scent of wildflowers in a spring rain.

"Right," Io says blinking. Her eyes dim a bit as she offers me a small smile.

As she turns to go I encircle her waist and draw her to me, pressing my lips to hers. Time stands still. A thousand years could pass before we come up for air. Io presses her hips to mine as I trail my fingers down her back. I pull away and press my forehead against hers, our breaths mingling as the cool night air swirls around us. Io runs a delicate hand over my chest. I tuck a strand of hair behind her ear. Io rests her head against my chest. I breathe deep in an attempt to calm my racing heart.

I take Io's hand in mine. She rises up on tip toes to brush her lips against mine. I feel a spark of electricity as she deepens the kiss. Warmth spreads through my chest and I stiffen as she runs her hand down my back. I rest my hands on her hips. Io slips her hands beneath my shirt. I groan against her soft lips as her fingers trace small circles along my bare skin.

I pull away before all sense deserts me. Our breaths rise like clouds in the cold black night. The moon bathes us in her soft white light. I take Io by the hand and we set off toward camp. A moment longer and I would not have been able to restrain myself. Io's hand fits perfectly in mine. I run my thumb along the back of her hand as we walk through the long grass.

I lead Io to the tent that I set up for her. "Goodnight," I say brushing my lips against her brow.

"Goodnight," Io says rising onto her toes to press her lips against my cheek.

Io slips into the tent. I head further down the row to my own tent. I slip my boots off and undress. I can still feel the lingering heat of Io's touch dancing along my bare back. I exhale as I lay down on my cot. I place my hands behind the back of my head and stretch my legs out. I close my eyes and dream of Io.

CHAPTER 10

IO

I lay in my cot thinking of that kiss. Rowan's lips on mine. His intoxicating scent of cedar and the sea. The hard plane of his chest. The feel of our hips pressed together. The hard length of him beneath his trousers. Warmth pools in my belly and I exhale. I pull the furs up to my chin. My last thought before I drift off is of Rowan.

I sleep deeply. My eyelids are heavy. I pry them open and they slide closed again as I glimpse the golden light of mid morning. I feel guilty about the hour before I remember that I was nearly murdered yesterday. I suppose I earned a few extra hours of sleep. I stretch my arms over my head as I take a deep breath. I exhale and push myself into a sitting position. My head throbs painfully and I squeeze my eyes shut for a few shallow breaths.

I slowly lower my legs to the ground. I rise, swaying slightly as I scan the tent for my pack. I find it propped up against a basket of wool blankets. I rummage around for a fresh set of under clothes. I peel off my shirt and walk over to a wash basin. I sigh contentedly as I splash warm water on my face and neck. I strip down and use a wash cloth to clean myself. I am shivering in by the time I finish scrubbing my skin clean. The water in my wash basin is a dull gray. I wring the wash cloth out and set it on the table. I slip into clean under garments and a fresh set of traveling clothes. I carry the wash basin outside to empty it.

The sunshine feels wonderful on my skin.

A cool breeze keeps the temperature comfortable. I tip the basin over, the water cascades onto the dew covered grass, bending green the blades ever so slightly. I return the basin to its table and set off to find some food. The camp is bustling with activity. A group of men is loading tents onto a wagon. I follow my nose to the cook tent where a few stragglers are grabbing a late breakfast.

"Good Morning, Sunshine," the cheery cook says in greeting.

"Good Morning," I return. "Am I too late for breakfast?"

"Just in time, my dear," he says with a kind smile.

He is a man of average height with creases around his gray eyes and laugh lines on the sides of his mouth. His curly black hair is tucked under a red knit cap, he has a close cropped beard. He hands me a wooden plate piled high with eggs, bacon, and a scoop of oatmeal sprinkled with cinnamon and raisins.

"Thank you," I say. "I'm Io."

"Pleased to meet you, Io," he replies. "I am, Finn, one of the castle cooks."

"Pleased to meet you, Finn," I say. "You are an excellent cook. You'll have to let me help you in the kitchens some time."

"I'd be honored," Finn says.

I find a spot by the fire and sit down to eat. I feel much better after several bites of eggs and oatmeal. I nibble on a strip of bacon as I watch people rush about breaking down the camp. When I finish my meal, I rise to return my plate and fork to Finn. I find a wash bin outside the cook tent. I scrub my plate and fork with hot soapy water and rinse them clean. A young woman with dark brown hair is packing clean dishes into a trunk. I place my dishes into the trunk. She smiles her thanks.

I decide to find Selene and ask if she needs help with anything. I spot Selene and Helena carrying armfuls of supplies to a wagon outside of their tent. Helena smiles at me as I approach.

"How can I help?" I ask.

"We have a few more boxes of tinctures and salves to load into the wagon," Helena says.

I duck into the tent and come face to face with Rowan. His eyes light up when he sees me. I feel my cheeks grow hot as my mind drifts to memories of last night.

"Good Morning," Rowan says, adjusting a large cauldron filled with medicinal odds and ends in his arms.

"Good Morning," I say with a small smile. "Need a hand?"

"I'd love to hold hands, just let me get this to the wagon," Rowan says with a wink.

I laugh and shake my head as he steps out of the tent. I crouch down to pick up a box full of tiny glass bottles with cork stoppers. I rise carefully and walk slowly to the wagon with my fragile load. I deposit my box on the wagon floor. Rowan brushes his hand against mine as I turn to head back to the tent. I take his hand in mine, giving it a gentle squeeze.

Our eyes meet and all sense deserts me as he gazes into my soul.

"Do you two love birds mind stepping aside? This box is rather heavy," Selene teases.

I startle and drop Rowan's hand. To my relief, Rowan takes no offense at my embarrassment. He places a hand on the small of my back as we step aside to clear a path. Selene smiles, she seems to approve of our intimacy. She sets down her box and gives my shoulder a gentle pat as she turns back to the tent.

"How are you feeling?" Rowan asks. He turns those hazel eyes on me and I know he will see right through any lie I offer to ease his mind.

"Everything hurts and I'm dying," I say.

"Not on my watch," Rowan says, scooping me up into his arms like a small child.

I gasp and laugh as he sets me gently on the edge of the wagon. He presses a warm kiss to my forehead.

"You rest here. I can take care of everything else," Rowan says.

"I'm fine. I can help," I protest, trying to rise.

"No, you need to take it easy. Now stay put," Rowan says leaning in to kiss me.

I feel a sudden heat spread from Rowan's lips to mine. The heat seeps into my skin and a sigh escapes my lips as the throbbing in my head decreases. I feel drowsy. Rowan finds a blanket in the wagon, he spreads it out on the floor and eases me down.

"No fair, you magicked me to sleep" I murmur as my eyes close.

"I'll be back to check on you," Rowan whispers next to my ear, I can feel the warm smile on his lips.

I drift off and dream.

I am standing in the middle of a meadow of dandelions and wildflowers. I can hear waves crashing in the distance. I follow the sound of the sea to a dirt path that runs through the meadow. I follow the path and see a tree line up ahead. As I draw nearer to the edge of the forest I hear drums and voices. I feel uneasy, a shiver runs down my spine. The daylight is fading fast. Fear tells me to turn back but, something draws me into the forest's embrace. The path cuts through the trees. The drums grow louder and I see a great bonfire through the trees.

"Ah, Io, at last. We've been waiting for you, my dear," a female voice says behind me.

I whip around to find a tall slender woman dressed in a deep blue gown embellished with glittering golden stars. Her skin is smooth and pale as milk. Her bright green eyes and long auburn hair seem to glow in the low light. Her lips, red as a rose's petals, curve up in a smile. My heart thunders in my chest and I struggle to find my voice. I feel like she can hear my frantic thoughts as she gazes at me.

"How do you know me?" I ask warily.

"I have known your family for generations," she says simply.

"Who are you?" I ask.

"I am Sorcha," she replies. "Come, the others are ready for you."

She turns and strides toward the bonfire. I

hasten after her, driven by curiosity. I follow Sorcha to a large clearing. The drums are near deafening here. I see several bare chested men beating large drums around the bonfire. Men and women dance around the flames. The men wear buckskin pants and colorful tunics. The women are dressed in vibrant gowns, crowns of flowers on their heads. I watch their flowing skirts swirl in the firelight as they twirl round and round with their lovers. Sorcha stops at a long wooden table near the fire. She picks up a goblet encrusted with rubies and sapphires. Sorcha approaches the fire with her bejeweled goblet and dips it into the flames. I stare as she draws the goblet out, her pale hand entirely unscathed, the goblet brimming with blue and gold flames.

My feet move of their own accord, closing the distance between us. Sorcha gives me a small smile and offers me the goblet. I reach out tentatively and touch it. It is cool to the touch. My skin is impervious to the heat and flames. My eyes flick to Sorcha and she winks at me. Emboldened, I take the goblet into my hands.

"Drink," Sorcha says.

I hesitate, Sorcha waits patiently. I swallow hard and bring the goblet to my lips. I close my eyes and drink the fire. I feel no pain as the flames pass my lips and slide down my throat. The drums cease and silence envelopes me. I exhale and open my eyes to find myself alone in the clearing. The bonfire crackles in front of me. I spin around looking for any sign of the revelry that I witnessed a moment ago. Even the table has vanished. I cannot find a single footprint on the ground.

A sudden burning in my chest doubles me over, the goblet falls to the ground as I clutch my chest. A scream tears out of me as I fall onto all fours. I press my hands into the damp earth and hot tears stream down my cheeks. A searing heat consumes me. I struggle to slow my breathing as I try to make sense of it all. My eyes widen in shock as I watch my skin blacken and turn to ash. I'm burning from the inside out.

My insides are burning. I gasp in agony as I surrender to the inferno. My skin is burning away. My throat burns, cutting off my anguished screams. I fall forward and flip onto my back. I writhe on the ground, fallen leaves tangling in my hair as I thrash about. My clothes have been reduced to ashes. I stare in horror as my skin transforms into iridescent obsidian scales. What is happening to me!?

My bones snap and twist. The pain is excruciating, my vision blurs as I fight to remain conscious. My limbs are growing longer. I jerk to my side when I feel a stabbing pain in my upper back. I manage to get onto all fours, my breathing ragged as waves of pain crash over me. My fingers are morphing into curved claws. The scales have spread all over my body. I am rising from the forest floor. I open my mouth to scream and an ear splitting roar echoes through the night. What was that? I've got to get out of here.

I am dangling above the forest floor. How did I get up here? I look around frantically for some rational explanation. My eye catches on a lake to my right that I did not notice before. I try to make my way over to the water's edge.

The trees rustle and creek as I move on unsteady legs. The burning pain has suddenly vanished and I breathe deeply. I crouch down to take a drink of water. I bring my face close to the water's surface and freeze at the sight of my reflection. A pair of golden eyes stares back at me. I take in the long snout, glittering black scales, and razor sharp teeth. I am a Dragon!? Another roar turns my blood to ice. I hiccup and a stream of orange fire ignites the elm tree in front of me. Oh shit. How do I change back? Why did I change at all?

I sit down heavily on my haunches and curl my spiked tail around me. I start to cry. Or whatever dragons do when they are having an emotional meltdown. A pair of leathery black wings fold around my massive form as I lay my head on my claws. A cloud of smoke rises from my nostrils as I sigh.

"Well aren't you a beauty," Sorcha says from across the bonfire.

I spring up onto all fours and open my wings. Change me back! What did you do to me?

"Easy, dear heart. I simply awakened your magic," Sorcha says in an annoying calm voice.

You can hear my thoughts?

"I can hear the thoughts of all the beasts of Caelen," Sorcha says.

I am no beast. I am a woman. Change me back!

"You will learn to control your gift in time. You must master your emotions. Quiet your mind. Envision what it is you want," Sorcha says as she approaches me.

Gift? I did not ask for a gift. Take it back!

"This is your destiny, Io. I cannot quell your fire, just as I cannot pluck the Moon from the Heavens," Sorcha says gently.

Why me? I am nobody. I have no great destiny.

"Sleep now, dear heart. You have found the path. It is time to walk it," Sorcha says with a smile as she fades into the darkness, a shower of twinkling golden stars shimmering in her wake.

I flap my wings in irritation, sending a whoosh of air that nearly blows the bonfire out. I curl up in front of the dying fire and rest my head on the ground. How am I supposed to sleep? I am a fucking dragon! Maybe if I close my eyes, I will wake up from this bizzare dream. Yes, it's only a dream. It can't be real. I close my scaly eyelids and pray that I wake up without claws and scales.

CHAPTER 11

ROWAN

I leave Io in the wagon and return to the tent. I hope that my magic eased the worst of her pain so that she can sleep peacefully. Helena carries the last box to the wagon. I start to dismantle the tent poles. Bran walks over with a blonde woman on his arm. *The flavor of the week.* I raise my eye brows at him and he smirks back.

"We are all packed and ready to depart," Bran says.

"Perfect. We are just about done here," I say stacking the poles in a neat pile.

Bran steps away from his lady to help me with the canvas. We fold it into a tight square and place the poles on top. I use a leather strap to bind everything into a tight bundle. Bran hoists it up onto his shoulder and carries it to the wagon. The blonde woman smoothes her skirt as she watches Bran. I glance toward the wagon to check on Io. She continues to sleep soundly. Bran returns with a small tincture in his hand. I recognize it at once, a blend of herbs that the healers prepare to prevent pregnancy. Bran slips it into the blonde woman's palm. She stashes it in a skirt pocket.

"I need to get back to help Finn," the woman says.

"I'll find you later," Bran says giving her bottom a squeeze.

She swats his hand away playfully and kisses him before she turns away. Bran watches her swaying hips as she walks away.

"Can't remember her name?" I ask when she is out of ear shot.

"I haven't the faintest idea," Bran says with

a sigh, gazing after his nameless flame with longing.

"You're terrible," I say flatly.

"Life is too short not to go after what you want, my friend," Bran says clapping me on the back.

"I'll keep that in mind," I say absently, my eyes drifting back to the wagon where Io sleeps.

"You have fallen in love with our lost Princess," Bran says following my gaze.

"She has my heart," I confirm.

"I am happy for you, my friend," Bran says turning toward me, fixing me with a meaningful gaze.

The corner of my mouth turns up ever so slightly, I clap him on the back as I step away. My Mother and the other healers are climbing into the wagon. I see Io stirring on the wagon floor. I turn away to mount my horse. I swing myself into the saddle, and kick my heels, urging my mare forward. Our convoy continues onward toward Caelen. The energy in the air is restless and excited, we are homeward bound.

The sun warms our backs as we gallop through the open fields on the outskirts of the city. We pass several merchants on horse drawn carts laden with vegetables and fruits to sell. A red fox leaps out of a covered wagon clutching a dead chicken by the neck, he darts under the cover of brambles, the man driving the cart is none the wiser. My mare reaches the crest of a hill and we get our first glimpse of Caelen. I breathe in the wild air as I take in my home. We have been gone for six months. A smile tugs at my lips as I scan the roof tops and high stone walls encircling the city. At the far end, perched atop a steep hill sits the Black Keep where King Eamon rules. *I hope Io is awake to see her homeland. How strange it must be to have no memory of your birth place. I will show her all that Caelen has to offer. The fields of wildflowers surrounding Emerald Lake, Obsidian Falls, the sea cliffs, and the Black Keep.*

Excited chatter echoes all around me, we

are all elated to be home. I spot King Eamon ahead of me, giving quiet instructions to a group of young squires. They nod eagerly in unison and kick their horses into a steady gallop. They are riding ahead to announce our return no doubt. The castle guards and servants will prepare a welcome home feast in our honor. The streets will be swept and cleared for our entry. A gaggle of young warriors can barely contain their excitement, they race ahead to the city gates. I catch King Eamon smiling after them.

Brigid rides alongside the good King, I can see tears glistening in her eyes. She has not set eyes on her homeland in 18 years. I look away to allow her privacy. The Healers's wagon rumbles along behind me. I turn my mare around to check on Io. When I come around to the back of the wagon, only my Mother and the other women stare back at me.

"She hopped out as soon as we crested the hill," my Mother says with a chuckle.

I shake me head as I turn away to search

for my Princess. I spot her running through the grass, her cloak forgotten and her wild tangle of raven hair streaming behind her. I take off after her, pulling up short so as not to scare her.

"Need a ride?" I ask with a smile.

Io slows and turns, fixing me with those warm brown eyes, full of wonder. Her smile illuminates her lovely face. This image will live forever in my memory, the woman I love, a Goddess among mortals. My breath catches, words escape me and I return her smile. I slow to a trot and reach my arm down to her. Io grasps my forearm and I lift her into the saddle behind me. A gasp escapes her as she settles into the saddle, wrapping her arms around my waist. I give my mare a gentle kick of my heels. We take off after the young warriors who have nearly reached the city gates. Io's proximity is intoxicating. My skin warms beneath her gentle touch. I fight to keep my breathing even.

The city gates loom over us as we approach. I feel Io tense behind me. I place my left hand over hers to comfort her.

"Welcome home," I say over my shoulder so only she can hear.

"Thank you," Io whispers in my ear.

I feel her breath on my neck and a shiver runs through me. Io tightens her hold on me as we come to a stop before the massive wooden gates. I recognize the guards on duty.

"Welcome back, Rowan," Gerard booms from his post on the left side of the gate. "My Lady, welcome to Caelen," Gerard says with a bow of his head.

"Gerard, may I present Princess Io Flynn," I say.

"My apologies, Princess," Gerard says falling to one knee before us.

"Please, rise good Sir. Thank you for welcoming me," Io says graciously.

Gerard rises and gives Io a reverent nod before he turns to his fellow guard. "Open the gates!" He shouts up to the men on the wall above.

The clinking of chains and a flurry of movement atop the wall precedes the creaking of the thick wooden doors as the gate slowly opens inward to permit us entry. The guards bow as we enter the bustling city streets. Io scans our surroundings with the wide eyes of a curious child. I point out various shops and food establishments that people frequent. Io listens intently as she takes all the sights in.

"I will give you a proper tour once you have settled in," I promise.

"I would love that. Thank you, Rowan," Io says with a small smile, her eyes bright.

It is nearly noon and the farmer's market is in full swing. The smell of freshly baked bread wafts from the baker's stall. A woman in a dingy apron arranges mince pies and sweet rolls on a wooden table. Children weave in and out of the crowd, shrieking with delight. The stall next to the baker has woolen scarves and cloaks. I scan the crowded street ahead of us, our young warriors have disappeared.

They must have reached the keep by now. A stand with colorful bouquets of flowers catches Io's eye. I stop by the stall so she can get a better look.

Io dismounts and the young woman at the stall offers a welcoming smile. Io reaches out to pluck a red rose from a bucket. She closes her eyes as she inhales the rose's scent. I hand the young woman a gold coin. She nods her thanks. Io meets my gaze, I lose myself in her eyes, time stands still.

An uproar from the gates makes Io jump, we turn to see King Eamon riding through the city gates with the rest of our warriors. Brigid is at the King's right, several Kingsguard surround them for protection. The Healers's wagon is close behind.

"Let's get you home," I say. I mount my horse and extend a hand down to Io. She takes it and I lift her gently into the saddle. Guards from the Black Keep are clearing the streets to make way for the royal procession. I press on towards the keep, Io wraps her arms around my waist. The clop of my mare's hooves echoes through the streets as we near the massive Black Keep atop Caelen's highest hill top. The draw bridge has been lowered, the keep's gates open wide to welcome us. I nod to the posted guards as we pass.

Io clutches my belt as we cross the draw bridge, she glances at the moat far below us and quickly turns her gaze forward. We enter the courtyard where several servants and families are waiting to greet the King and loved ones who have been dearly missed. I can hear Io's shallow breaths, the tension rolls off her in anxious waves.

"Don't worry, I'll get you inside," I say giving her hand a gentle squeeze.

Io gives me a stiff nod as she exhales. The anxiety on her face melts away as she smooths her expression into a mask of serenity. I smile at her and she returns it with a brave smile of her own. I dismount, Io slides to the ground beside me before I can offer her my hand. A few of the maids raise their eyebrows in surprise. Io is dressed in simple traveling pants, a tunic, and leather boots. Her wind blown hair falls to the middle of her back. Io stands tall as she flashes the women a winning smile. I lead our mount to the stables at the south end of the keep. Io walks beside me with her head held high. The maids whisper behind their hands as we pass. A mischievous grin plays on Io's lips, she reaches her hand over and grabs my behind with a firm grip. I startle at the forward gesture, the corners of my mouth twitching. At the sight of this, the oldest maid claps her hand over her mouth, the two young maids giggle with glee.

"You do love to make an impression," I say clearing my throat as Io withdraws her palm. I flash her a grin.

"I do enjoy ruffling the hens's feathers," Io replies as she glances over her shoulder, shooting the maids a cheeky wink.

We snicker as we continue on toward the stables. Once we are out of earshot, Io relaxes considerably. She studies the Black Keep against a pale blue sky. The sun is beginning to sink into the sea, the light stains the clouds orange and pink. Io's upturned face is illuminated by the setting sun. *The sky itself is jealous of her face.*

CHAPTER 12

IO

Caelen is not what I expected. The sprawling city is immaculate-not a thing out of place, not a single beggar in sight, the buildings and homes are painted in vibrant colors, the city folk seem kind, and the Black Keep sits atop Caelen's highest hill top. A farmer's market right inside the city gates is teeming with life, people young and old selling fresh fruits and vegetables, freshly baked bread from a stone fire oven, luxurious scarves and cloaks, and a stall over flowing with beautiful, fragrant blooms.

Rowan draws his mare up to the stall. I slide from the saddle and the young woman tending the stall smiles warmly at me. I reach for a red rose, the petals are soft as silk and the scent is divine. Rowan presses a gold coin into the young woman's palm.

I feel a shiver run down my spine as we ascend the hill. This is the home of my ancestors. The midnight black stone and tall, looming towers draw my eye, I feel their eerie call deep in my bones. Curiosity quells my fear. I feel as though I have been here before, in a long forgotten dream. Rowan nods to the black clad guards posted at the drawbridge. The horse's hoof beats reverberate off the high stone walls surrounding the Black Keep. I glance down at the perilous drop to the rushing waters far below. I feel my stomach churn and a sheen of sweat coats my clammy skin. I shift my eyes to stare straight ahead.

We pass through the gates and find ourselves in a large courtyard. I take in the sprawling green lawn dotted with large shrubs and flowering trees. A crowd of servants and families of the warriors have assembled outside to greet us. Rowan dismounts. I slip from the saddle before he can offer me a chivalrous hand. Many of the servants are eyeing me, a group of three women are whispering furiously behind their hands, casting furtive glances my way. *The castle gossips. I'll give them something to talk about.*

Rowan leads our sweet mare to the stables. I quicken my steps to draw right up alongside him, I run my left hand down his lower back to his firm buttocks and give him a rather suggestive squeeze. The oldest of the maids claps her hand over her mouth in horror. The two young maids succumb to a fit of giggles.

"You do love to make an impression," Rowan says clearing his throat, he regards me with a grin.

"I do enjoy ruffling the hens's feathers," I reply, shooting the maids a cheeky wink.

Rowan and I lock eyes, the shimmering

flecks of gold in his hazel eyes still my heart. We snicker as we walk, desperately trying to wipe our amusement from our faces. I feel the tension seeping from my body as we round the corner of the keep. The sun hangs low in the sky, coloring the fluffy clouds on the horizon orange and pink. *My first sunset in Caelen.*

We reach the royal stables. Young stable hands tend to weary horses, gently removing dusty saddles and pouring cupfuls of water over their aching backs. The horses snort quietly as their care takers brush their bodies and manes. The stalls have been mucked, fresh hay spread on the packed dirt floor. Rowan finds an empty stall for the mare.

"I forgot to ask her name," I say, loosening a cinch on the saddle.

"Nyx," Rowan says, running a hand lovingly down her neck.

"A perfect name," I say, stroking Nyx's sleek black coat. "Thank you for carrying us home, Nyx."

Nyx nudges my hand with her nose in acknowledgement. Rowan lifts the saddle from Nyx's back. She neighs in delight. I find a bucket of water with a wooden cup in the corner of the stall. I pour a cupful of water over Nyx's back. The water is warm and Nyx lets out a snort of relief. Rowan watches me as I tend to her.

"You have a way with horses," Rowan says reverently.

"I prefer animals to most people," I joke.

"I understand," Rowan says with a chuckle. "If you can stand my company a bit longer, I would like to escort you to the feast."

"I'll allow it," I say, meeting his steady gaze.

Rowan smiles, taking the wooden cup from me, his fingers brush the back of my hand and I feel the simmering heat of his fire. He sets the wooden cup aside and slowly brushes Nyx's body. I look down to my dusty boots and soiled traveling clothes.

"Would it be possible to have a bath before the feast?" I ask self consciously.

"I will show you to your quarters," Rowan says. "I am sure the maids will be anxious to meet you, Your Grace."

"I'm sure they will be rather disappointed," I say with a sigh.

Rowan places a hand under my chin, raising it slightly to meet my gaze. "I highly doubt that."

His words send ripples of liquid fire through my body and I feel weak in the knees. The intensity of his stare makes me feel exposed and naked, as though he can see my very soul. My desire for this man, my valiant protector who wields fire and heals with his tender touch, will be my undoing. *I surrender.*

Rowan withdraws his hand, the absence of his touch leaves me with a deep ache in my chest. I blink my eyes and take a steading breath before I follow Rowan out of the stables. We walk around the corner of the stables and find ourselves in a lush garden. The scent of basil, rosemary, mint, lavender and sage fill the air. Each plant is identified by hand painted wooded signs. There are rows of carrots, potatoes, sweet peppers, tomatoes, cucumbers, greens, celery, pumpkins, and onions. Succulent strawberries, blueberries, raspberries, and melons flourish in large garden beds. Fruit trees are loaded with lemons, oranges, apples, and peaches. A green pasture on out right has goats, sheep, and cows. There is a large chicken coop next to the rows of vegetables.

Up ahead there is a small wooden door. Rowan opens the door and I step through. We are in the kitchens. *Finally, a place I am comfortable.* The cooks do not look up from their cooking as we pass. The clang of cast iron pots, the scraping of wooden spoons, and the crackling fire are sounds of comfort to me. Long wooden prep tables are laid with baskets of warm bread, roasted pumpkin, platters of roast beef, several roast chickens, mashed potatoes, fresh greens with tomatoes and cucumbers, and a large cauldron of onion soup. My stomach grumbles.

We exit the kitchen and follow a stone corridor up to another level of the keep, torches set into the stone walls light our way. We pass a few wooden doors with large iron handles. I try to memorize our route so I know how to slip out through the kitchens undetected. At the end of the corridor we ascend a spiral staircase. My legs start to ache and sweat beads on my brow from exertion. Just when I think I can go no further, we reach the landing.

We are in a great hall with high vaulted ceilings, polished stone floors, and enormous stained glass windows windows depicting all sorts of creatures. My eye is drawn to a shimmering black dragon breathing fire. Servants are rushing back and forth, setting the long tables with silverware and cloth napkins, arranging flowers in glittering vases, and carrying platters of food from the kitchens. Rowan and I weave through the frantic crowd.

We cross the hall to a large archway which opens to yet another stone corridor guarded by warriors in black, one massive man with flaxen hair and a tall slender woman with black hair done up in intricate braids.

"Welcome back, Rowan," the woman says in a friendly tone as we approach.

"Hello, Ravena," Rowan replies. "I present her royal highness, Princess Io Flynn."

Both warriors fall to one knee, flushing my cheeks with embarrassment.

"Your Grace," the warriors say in reverent unison.

"Please rise," I say. "Thank you for welcoming me."

"I will alert the servants to your presence, Princess," Ravena says with a bow of her head.

"Welcome home, Your Grace. I am Darren. I am a member of the Royal Guard," the burly warrior says.

"I am pleased to meet you both. I look forward to seeing you around the Keep," I say bowing my head.

Rowan places a hand on the small of my back as he leads me away from the guards. He is careful to keep some distance between our bodies. I appreciate his consideration and care. *He makes me feel safe.* Rowan withdraws his hand when we reach a large oak door. Rowan turns the handle and enters. He motions for me to wait on the threshold while he sweeps the rooms. When he is satisfied he comes back to my side.

"All clear. These are your personal chambers," Rowan says.

I take a tentative step into the sitting room. Back in Greenwood my Mother and I shared a modest room in the servants quarters. This sitting room is three times the size of my old room. The thick carpets are embroidered with deep blue roses. A crimson sofa is decorated with golden, tasseled pillows. Someone has lit a roaring fire in the large hearth. A mahogany table has been set for tea, steam curls from the spout of a porcelain teapot. A tray of sandwiches and red apples calls to my growling stomach.

"Your sleeping quarters are just through there," Rowan indicates an archway with hanging twinkling, golden beads.

Rowan plucks a turkey sandwich from the tray and wanders over to the hearth. I peek into the bedroom under the archway. A decadent four poster bed veiled by indigo curtains sits at the center of the room. Another hearth is set into the far wall, the warmth seeps into my bones. To the left of the hearth is a balcony that overlooks the gardens and the sea beyond the city walls. There are several bookshelves with leather bound books, a small pale blue sofa with cream colored cushions, and a writing desk with a high backed chair. To the right of the hearth stands a large copper tub with steaming water. I nearly faint at the sight of it. *At last!*

I return to the sitting room. Rowan is standing at the hearth eating his sandwich. He turns at the sound of my footsteps, covering his mouth with a calloused hands. He swallows a mouthful before he speaks.

"My apologies, I was famished," Rowan says with a sheepish look.

"No, please help yourself," I say with a wave of the hand.

"I'll let you get ready. We will have guards posted at your door, Rowan says. "I can be back in an hour to escort you to the great hall."

"That would be lovely," I say with a smile. Rowan smiles back before he turns to take his leave.

"Rowan," I call out before I can stop myself.

Rowan pauses to look back at me. I take a step toward him. Rowan slowly closes the distance between us, our breaths mingle together. He reaches for my hand as he tucks some hair behind my ear. I press my body against his. Rowan leans down as I press up into his warm lips. Fire spreads from my face down to my belly. Rowan wraps his arms around me, cradling my to his broad chest, the hard plane of his stomach. My breath hitches and a small sigh escapes my lips. Rowan pulls away, gently holding the small of my back.

"I better go before I lose myself," Rowan says with a crooked smile.

"I'll see you soon," I say with a wink.

Rowan laughs, "Not soon enough, Princess."

He steps back with a bow. I watch the sway of his muscled form as he walks to the door. I shake my head as I turn back toward the waiting tub. *Quite the day.*

CHAPTER 13

ROWAN

It takes every ounce of self control to force my feet away from Io. The fire of her lips, still burning on mine as I close the door behind me. I retrace our steps back down the west wing corridor, nodding to Ravena and Darren when I pass beneath the archway. I take a right and head for the corridor to the guards quarters. I pass a few friends in the corridor, barely hearing their greetings and small talk. I am still savoring the Io's heat when I find my chamber door. A fire has been set in my hearth. *Thank you, Cor-*

mac. Many officers have pages assigned to help them with housekeeping and minor errands. *A perk that feels unnecessary, in my opinion. I have learned to appreciate the help though.*

I pull my filthy shirt over my head and drop it to the floor. Cormac has filled the tub with steaming hot water from the kitchens. I loosen my trousers and kick off my boots. I peel off my soiled socks and add them to the discard pile. I step into the tub, I sigh as I sink into the hot bath. A small side table holds a fresh bar of rosemary peppermint soap and a wash cloth. I scrub the dirt off my skin, brown water runs down my chest and forearms. I sink beneath the water for a moment to rinse my hair. I close my eyes and see Io's face.

When I emerge from the bath, the water is a dull grey. I grab a towel from the side table and wrap it around my waist. I cross the room to open the window. Cormac has left a small bucket next to the tub. I fill the bucket with the bath water and carry it over to the window. I glance down to the rocks below before emptying the contents of my bucket. The water plummets to the craggy rocks below. My room has a perfect view of the sea cliffs that the Black Keep perches on. I gaze out at the horizon where the last golden rays of sunlight have slipped into the churning sea. I repeat this process several times until the tub is emptied. Cormac would have done this while I was at the feast but, I do not like him to clean up after me. The young lad deserves to enjoy his night as well.

I collect my dirty clothes and deposit them into a basket at the foot of my bed. I pull open the door of my wardrobe to search for something to wear. Many noble men and high ranking military officials indulge in opulent garments. I am quite the opposite. I pull on a plain pair of black trousers, slip on a black under shirt, and locate a fresh pair of socks. I select my favorite leather jerkin and find a clean pair of leather boots.

I buckle my sword belt and slip my dagger into my right boot. I exit my chambers, making my way back to Io. A pair of gossiping maids pass me in the stone corridor, engrossed in some castle scandal. One is wrinkled with white curls and a plump figure. Her companion, decades younger with a slight frame and chestnut brown hair, cropped short. I recognize them from the kitchens and washroom. They nod as I pass. I return the gesture without breaking my stride.

When I reach Io's chambers, I knock on the heavy oak door. A middle aged maid answers, stepping aside to permit my entry.

"Thank you, my Lady," I say.

"Of course, my Lord. The Princess awaits you," she replies, gesturing to the sitting room.

When I step into the sitting room, my breath catches in my throat. Io is standing at the window, dressed in a flowing gown of forest green. A skilled seamstress has painstakingly stitched a lovely pattern of roses and leaves with golden thread across the full skirt. The fitted bodice has golden laces at the back, cinching Io's narrow waist and accentuating her slender figure. Long flowing sleeves of a sheer forest green material hang down from her wrists. Io's hair has been braided in an intricate style, several locks have been left loose, cascading down her back. Io turns at the sound of my footsteps.

"Hello stranger," Io says with a small smile. "I tired to get ready quickly. I did not want to keep you waiting."

"You are radiant," I say, watching her smooth her skirts nervously.

"It's a bit much," Io says shifting uncomfortably from one foot to the other. "The maids insisted that wearing my traveling clothes would be inappropriate. I think they had them burned."

I laugh and Io joins me, her laughter is like tinkling wind chimes in a summer breeze. Her golden brown eyes sparkle when she laughs. I offer her my arm, Io takes it with a delicate hand. We step out into the corridor. As we near the great hall, the strumming of lutes and sweet bard song reaches our ears. The ghost of a smile lingers on Io's lips. She holds her head high as we enter the bustling hall. King Eamon's table has been set up in front of his throne. Several curious ladies and gentlemen of the court crane their necks to gawk at Io as we pass. Io pays them no mind, she is absolutely stunning, a vision in green. I spy several women making sour faces at the sight of her. *Court is no place for a gentle soul like Io. These vultures will try to pick her apart. I will not let that happen.*

We reach the King's table, I pull a seat out at the King's right side for Io. Brigid is seated on the King's left. I take a seat at Io's right. The mood in the hall is light and joyful. Couples twirl on the dance floor, a blur of vibrant skirts and sashes. The music reverberates off the vaulted ceiling, long silk fabrics hang from the exposed wooden beams, aerialists perform acrobatic feats high above our heads. Io gazes at them in wonder. Hand balancers and jugglers perform on the ground beneath them. An impressive spread has been laid out, the Kitchen staff have truly out done themselves. Roast chickens, crisp, browned turkeys, mince meat pies, stews, soups, and platters of roasted root vegetables, fresh greens with cucumbers and tomatoes, and bowls of fresh berries with cream, puddings, and pastries cover the long center tables. Servers file between the tables refilling goblets with spiced mead and wine. Large glass pitchers of water are set upon every table. My stomach rumbles when I breathe in all the savory aromas.

"Welcome to Caelen, Io," King Eamon says with a warm grandfatherly smile.

"Thank you, Your Grace," Io says returning his smile.

I can see him in her face. The golden flecks in her eyes are identical to the golden flecks in his green eyes. Her smile is a mirror of his own. They have the same gentle soul with a simmering fire hidden just beneath the surface. I have seen King Eamon set a child on his knee and sever the limbs off men on the field of battle. Anyone foolish enough cross him after mistaking his kindness for weakness, will be reduced to ash. I have not known Io as long but, I have a sense that there is more to her than I know. I have never been more intrigued to uncover someone's soul.

A passing server fills our goblets with spiced mead. I take a sip, the warm liquid calms my nerves. I scan the crowd for any threat of danger, a habit that I cannot quite shake. I remind myself to ask the King about training Io in self defense. Here in Caelen, young girls train alongside boys in the arts of war. The youth fortunate enough to be born with a magical gift are highly sought after. After my Father died, my Mother came to King Eamon's court, in hopes of finding a safe life for us. King Eamon was kind, he offered his condolences to my Mother, he listened to her plea for help. She asked if the good King would take me on as a squire, give me a safe place to live and food to eat. He told my Mother that he would not separate a Mother from her son. He offered her a place at Court as a Healer. My Mother worked at an Apothecary in the city. Men and Women sought her out for her healing gift and magical tinctures. King Eamon had heard of her kind heart and healing hands.

A flash of movement at the corner of my eye turns my head. The server who poured our mead...she slipped a small glass vial into her pocket. I look down to my goblet and turn to the King as he raises his goblet to his lips. I shoot my hand out and knock the goblet from his hand. The King startles and looks to me for an explanation. The smashing of a pitcher turns all of the heads at the table to the serving girl who has dropped her pitcher and sprinted off into the crowd. I leap over the table, upsetting a tureen of pumpkin carrot soup as I hit the stone floor running. The girl is dressed in a plain rough spun blue kitchen dress with a white apron. Her blonde hair is in a plait down her back, it swings wildly as she shoves guests out of the way to clear a path. I whistle to the guards at the far end of the hall. They bar the doors and shout for the guards at the three other exits to do the same. The girl pivots to the right, barreling towards the grand staircase that leads to the keep's library and observatory. I am closing in on her, I reach out and snag her by the braid. A scream tears out of her small body and she kicks like a wild beast. I pin her to my chest and wrestle her to the ground. Footsteps pound behind me and five castle guards arrive on the scene.

"Let me go!," she shrieks. "I didn't do anything!"

"Then why run?" I ask, holding her hands in a vice like grip.

"She made me do it!" the girl shouts between ragged breaths.

"Who made you do what?"

"Lady Terra," she pants. "She told me if I did not poison the King that she'd kill me family." She dissolves into loud heaving sobs.

I heave her to her feet and pass her over to

a guard. "Take her to the dungeons. Find Terra."

"Aye, Captain," the young guard says with a nod. He binds the girls hands before he and two other guards lead her away.

The remaining two rush off to find the Lord Commander's daughter. I make my way back toward the King's table. The Kingsguard have surrounded the table with their swords drawn. Servers and castle guards are ushering the guests outside. People are craning their necks to get a look at the King's table. All manner of wild theories spilling from their flapping lips. I let out a heavy sigh. I did not even get to set a plate. I shake my head to clear it. Back to the matter at hand. The Kingsguard step aside as I approach the table.

"What have you found out?" King Eamon asks.

"The girl claims that Terra Kade threatened to kill her family if she did not poison you, Your Grace," I say.

"Thank you, Rowan," King Eamon says gravely, grasping my shoulder.

I merely nod. A castle guard gingerly picks up the fallen goblet. The puddle of spiced mead on the carpet is bubbling, wisps of pungent purple smoke are rising from the liquid. My Mother stands a safe distance away examining it.

"Nightshade," she states. "Extremely deadly. A mere three drops is fatal."

"Bring the Lord Commander and his daughter to the dungeons for questioning," King Eamon says with a snarl.

"At once, Your Grace. Guards have already been dispatched."

I bow and hurry off to see to the Lord Commander personally. I catch Io's eye as I turn. She offers a grim smile. I give her a wink as I pass. The corners of her lips turn up slightly. I feel a warmth blooming in my chest as I take off running, my fellow Kingsguard at my heels. The men and ladies of the Court are drifting back to their quarters, common folk are leaving the Black Keep through the North gate. The Lord Commander has a tower near the west side of the castle grounds. Forty Kingsguard are moving in on the tower as we approach. An ear splitting boom shatters the quiet night, throwing me from my feet. I fly backwards, hitting the ground with such force that the breath is forced from my lungs. Screams and shouts fill the air. The smell of burning flesh makes me gag. I struggle up to a sitting position, my head pounds, every muscle in my body protesting my commands. I stagger to my feet. The Lord Commander's tower is engulfed in scarlet flames, the color of House Kade. The forty Kingsguard who arrived before us, have been reduced to a mere ten. Bodies and limbs litter the lawn. The carnage is enough to turn the toughest man to a sniveling coward.

The ten survivors stumble around in a daze. One man is clutching the stub of his left arm, holding the severed left forearm in his right hand. I take him by the shoulders and sit him down on the grass. He stares blankly ahead, his face as white as a ghost. I remove his belt and make a tourniquet just above his left elbow joint. My Mother and her Healers arrive on the scene. She spots me and I see the relief in her terror stricken eyes.

"Hurry!" I shout. "We have heavy casualties!"

My Mother shouts orders and her women obey. Women dressed in simple sage green gowns dash forward to help. Their faces serene and unaffected by the carnage. They set to work helping all they can. Men screaming like frightened children with tears streaming down their faces cling to every word falling from the lips of their healing angels. *Freya save them.*

I look back toward the tower. Several hooded figures slip into the trees beyond the tower. There is a path that leads down to the beach. I grab ten men and we silently pursue. One figure appears to be the Lord Commander Kade. A smaller, slight figure appears to be Terra. The third, I can only venture a guess as to who that might be. Judging from the size and movements it is a male warrior. A personal guard, perhaps. We fan out and surround the party. My men slip through the dark wood like deathly shadows, closing in on their prey. At my signal our archer loses an arrow. It zips through the air, the Lord Commander turns a moment too late and it sinks deep into his shoulder. Terra screams and takes off running. All hell breaks loose. The large warrior lunges at her, tackling her to the ground. She screams in fury, swinging wildly, tearing his hood off to reveal dark brown, short cropped hair. *Kellan, Terra's betrothed.*

Kellan is one of Lord Commander Kade's personal guard. He is ten years Terra's senior, a vicious ale soaked man with a fondness for beating women. Even a woman as vile as Terra deserves better than the likes of him. I come up from behind and slash at Kellan's back, he howls in rage as a stream of crimson splatters my face. He turns on me, the pain etched on his face, tells me that I cut deep. He fumbles for his blade. I don't give him the chance. I drive my sword into his belly. Kellan's mouth opens wide, he falls forward, I push him away as I wrench my sword free with a sickening squelch. Terra vomits all over herself, to my amusement. I tower over her.

"Wait! Please!" She screams, holding her open hands up in surrender. Her eyes wide as saucers, her blonde hair stuck to the snot running from her nose.

"You have three seconds," I spit.

"It was my Father! I had nothing to do with it!"

"You expect me to believe that you were ignorant of his intentions?"

"I am no murderer," she says, her eyes burning into mine with defiance.

"It is out of my hands."

Terra scrambles to her feet, flinging a dagger at my chest before she turns and flees. It slashes my upper left arm as I dive out of the way. I curse myself for even letting her speak. I sprint after her and tackle her to the ground. She twists and bites my hand viciously. I grunt and grab the back of her hair. She howls and claws at my face. I fight the urge to back hand her. Instead I pin her arms behind her and wrench her to her feet. I taste blood at the corner of my mouth where a trail of blood ran down my cheek from a deep scratch. I drag her back to the Great Hall.

When we enter, ten castle guards run forward to bind her hands and bring her before the King. Terra puts up a vicious fight, kicking one guard in the groin and punching another in the nose. The men roughly drag her to the King's table after stripping her of another dagger hidden in her boot and a wicked curved blade that was hidden in her belt. King Eamon's face of stone gives her pause. She cowers beneath his gaze.

"What do you have to say for yourself, child?"

"It was my Father, I swear." Her eyes hold

the King's withering glare and I examine her face closely.

Terra straightens and lifts her chin so that the King can search her eyes. The moment stretches and the guards hold her still, waiting for their King's command. King Eamon glances at me, I give him an imperceptible nod. He turns back to the captive.

"If what you say is true, you will help us apprehend your Father. If you are found to be false, you will be put to the sword."

"He has a secret lair in a cave below the sea cliffs. There is an underwater entrance beneath the Dragon's Tooth. When the tide is low, it is exposed for a short time."

Terra's face shows the shame of her betrayal. In her eyes, the naked fear of a wild animal who has been cornered with no escape. Io steps forth, I move to join her but, she holds her hand out.

"Why should we trust you?"

"What choice do you have?" Terra fires back.

Io strides forward and punches her in the face. Terra's head snaps to the left and she reels from the surprisingly devastating blow. She spits a mouthful of blood on the floor. Io grabs her by the front of her soiled red gown and glares into her shocked ice blue eyes.

"Your very life is in my hands. Disrespect me again," Io whispers in a deadly voice.

Terra swallows. Io shoves her back into the guards hands. The guards force her to her knees. Terra has the good sense to bow her head and shut her cursed mouth. Io turns and walks past her, heading in the direction of the royal chambers. I look to King Eamon for guidance. I am not surprised to see a suppressed smile on his lips for the briefest of moments before his stony expression returns.

"Take her to the dungeons," King Eamon commands. "If she is lying, she will be dealt with swiftly."

Terra blinks back tears as the guards take her away. The fight seems to have gone out of her. She allows them to lead her away, resigned to her fate.

CHAPTER 14

IO

I hope that no one can see my hands shaking as I stride away from a disheveled Terra. *So much for making a good impression at my first royal function.* I realize that I made a wrong turn somewhere. This is not the way back to my chambers. *Great, now I'm lost.* I let out a long sigh. I have stumbled upon an unfamiliar corridor with a red carpet and a large stained glass window depicting a black dragon. *That's not unsettling.*

"That is my favorite window."

I jump and knock over a large glass vase

full of red roses. Rowan dives for the vase, saving it before it smashes to pieces on the stone floor. He sets it gently back in place on the table beneath the window. My heart is in my throat, my hands shaking uncontrollably.

"I am sorry, I did not mean to scare you," Rowan says, keeping his distance.

"I'm fine," I manage with a rather unconvincing smile.

"It is ok to not be ok."

Rowan peers at me with those hazel eyes. I feel that there is nothing I could ever hide from him. *Maybe I don't want to? Maybe I want him to see all of me.* I swallow and look down at my hands.

"Why the dragon?"

"The Dragon is the sigil of House Flynn," Rowan explains.

I have at the strangest feeling that I have been here before. Rowan moves closer to me as I examine the painted glass. I flinch when I feel a hand on my shoulder. I turn to look up at Rowan. *Something is not right.* There is no warmth at his touch. I stiffen, dread pools in my stomach as I meet his eyes. They have shifted to an *icy blue.*

"What the-?"

A sharp pain on the left side of my neck cuts me off. The scream is trapped in my throat as I struggle to make sense of what I am seeing. A white snake is slithering down my left shoulder, winding down my trembling arm and wrapping around a pale, slender outstretched arm. *Rowan has transformed into Terra*. The room tilts and I sway on my feet, the ground rushes up to meet me. I collapse to the red carpet, gasping for breath, my vision narrows as I struggle to rise.

"Don't fight it," Terra says in a gentle voice. Her voice sounds far away. "Let the venom spread."

"What did you-?"

Terra kneels down beside me as my thrashing movements begin to slow. The world starts to fade. My mind is screaming in panic but, my body cannot respond to my desperate pleas to fight.

"I'll see you beyond the Veil, *Princess.*"

Terra's derisive laughter echoes throughout the blackness as I go under. The sound of her receding footsteps pound in my ears. Rowan's face swims before me. *I wish I could have kissed him, one last time.*

I am floating through the darkness. The cold has seeped deep into my bones. I slowly open my eyes. My vision is blurry and distorted. The world is silent. I raise my hand to rub my eyes and I feel the swish of water. *I am under water.* I look around frantically. A flash of light over head catches my attention. I kick hard with my legs as I draw the water down with long sweeps of my arms. The flashes of lightning in the sky above grow brighter as I draw nearer to the surface. My right hand breaks the surface as I feel a strong downward tug on my left ankle. Panic sets in as I look down to see a gray scaly hand gripping my left ankle. A set of glowing green eyes stare up at me. I thrash to free myself from the creature's inhuman grasp. I still as five more pairs of glowing green eyes materialize in the murky depths. My heart hammers in my chest, I fight to remain calm. *This is not where I will meet my end.*

I aim a kick at the creature's face, feeling a satisfying crunch as my boot connects with sinew and bone. A sharp screeching sound reverberates through the water as I shoot upward. I burst through the surface, sputtering and coughing. I scramble to the shore, clawing for purchase along the muddy bank.

"Took you long enough."

I spin around to find a bored looking Terra sitting beneath a large tree with strange blood red flowers. She is cleaning mud from beneath her fingernails with the tip of a bejeweled dagger. I stomp over and shove her roughly against the tree.

"What the fuck didi you do to me!? Where are we?"

Terra shoves me backward, brandishing

her dagger. "Do you really want to know? Or should we just roll around in the mud while our lives hang in the balance?"

"You are the reason we're here in the first place! Explain!"

"We are in the Underworld," Terra says simply as though no further explanation is needed.

I scowl at her annoyingly calm demeanor and gesture for her to continue.

"It seems we may be of use to each other. We are both searching for people we love. I know the way back. We will need to work together to survive."

"What are you talking about? Speak plainly." I growl.

"Rowan is here. You must get him back to the Land of the Living before sunrise."

"You killed Rowan?" I seethe. I grip her pale throat and squeeze until her eyes bulge. "You vile, bitch!"

I throw her to the ground and kick her in

the stomach. Terra curls into a ball, bracing for another attack.

"Get up! Where is Rowan?" I scream.

"I don't know," Terra groans.

"You don't seem very useful," I snarl. "Who are you trying to save?"

"My-friend," Sara says hesitantly.

I pause, exhaling through my nose to calm myself. I refuse to feel any sympathy for this witch. I step back to give her room to stand. Terra slowly rises to her feet, wincing slightly.

"How do we find them?"

"We must walk the path to the City of the Dead. That is where all wayward souls end up."

"Lead the way," I say.

"You trust me?" Terra asks raising her eyebrows.

"Never. I just don't have much of a choice," I say scowling.

"Fair enough. Let's go," Terra says, tossing her blonde hair over her shoulder.

Terra steps around the tree she was

leaning against. I gasp as I take in the landscape before us. A long dirt road stretches to the horizon, the surrounding land is desolate, red sand dunes and dead skeletal trees as far as the eye can see. In the distance I can just make out a sprawling city. My heart lifts when I spot a set of fresh footprints. They could be Rowan's. I follow Terra. *I'm going to regret this. But she is my best hope to find Rowan.*

We walk in silence. The sky is a dismal grey, thunder rumbles, and purple flashes of lightning split the sky. It is impossible to tell what time of day it might be, maybe time does not matter here.

"Are we both dead?"

"Not yet," Terra replies. "We must make it back to the lake and return to our world before sunrise."

"What happens if we don't?"

"Then we spend eternity here."

"Marvelous," I sigh.

A gust of wind whips red sand against the side of my face, stinging my cheek. I shield my eyes with my hand as we trudge on. *This is impossible. How will I find Rowan and get back to this lake in time?* I quicken my pace. There is no time to despair. I will have to watch my back. Terra cannot be trusted. I will tolerate her until I find Rowan. Then we'll race back to the lake.

CHAPTER 15

ROWAN

When Io does not answer the door to her chambers, I let myself in after the fourth knock, careful to keep my eyes on the floor in case she is not dressed. My stomach twists when I realize that the chamber is empty. The hearth has burned down to glowing embers. The sitting room is exactly as we left it. There is no sign that she has returned to the chamber. I exit quickly. *Something is wrong. Io where are you?*

She may have gotten turned around. I search the intersecting corridors. I break into a run, skidding to a halt when I catch a glimpse of dark green. There at the end of the corridor beneath a massive stained glass window, lays my Princess. My heart stops and I rush over to her still form. Io is lying on her side, her black hair covering her face. I pull her into my lap, smoothing her hair away from her face.

"Io? Wake up. Io!"

I feel a warm trickle run down my wrist, there is a nasty bite on the left side of her neck. The puncture wounds are deep, the surrounding skin a bright angry red. I check her pulse, it is alarmingly weak. Her lovely face has grown deathly pale. *I should have been here.*

I clench my hands into fists and close my eyes. I slip my arm beneath her legs and draw her close to my chest as I rise. I need to get her help. I rest Io's head against my chest and head back to the Great Hall.

"She won't wake."

I snap my head to the right to find Terra

sitting in a plush chair by the window. I clench my jaw and exhale as I turn to face her.

"What did you do?" I demand.

"Fear not, Sir Rowan, I will tell you how to save your Beloved."

I gently lower Io to the floor before I round on the wretch. The smug smile slips from Terra's face, her eyes grow wide with fear as I close in on her. She jumps to her feet but, I foil her escape easily, snatching her right wrist. A small gasp escapes her as I throw her to the ground and place my boot on her chest.

"WHAT DID YOU DO!?"

"You'll never wake her without me," Terra grunts as she squirms beneath my boot.

"TELL ME NOW!"

"I sent her to the Underworld! You will have to follow and bring her back before sunrise."

I stomp on her chest and her head knocks against the stone floor. Her eyes glaze over for a moment, her mouth gaping as the breath whooshes out of her. I seize the front of her dress, hauling her to her feet. She sways on the spot. I shove her back into the chair. She plops down heavily clutching her chest.

"You cracked my rib, asshole!" She says through gritted teeth.

"That's the least of your worries. How do I get to Io?"

"You have to die."

"Do your worst, bitch."

Terra glares at me, the corners of her crimson lips curving up into a wicked smile. She closes her eyes and extends her left arm out, palm up. A gleaming white snake emerges from the bell sleeve of her red gown. The snake slithers down to her open palm, watching me with icy blue eyes. I extend my right arm out. The snake leaves her Mage, winds up my arm. I suppress a shiver as the snake pauses at the side of my neck.

"Time to test your love," Terra sneers.

The snake strikes, pain blooms on the side of my neck where the fangs sank deep. The venom seems to have turned my veins to ice. I stagger a step and fall heavily to my knees. My breathing is labored and my vision clouds.

"Find Io and bring her back before the sun touches the highest tower of the Black Keep."

"How will I bring her back?" I slur.

"Love will show you the way."

I fall backward, my heartbeat slowing as I am dragged down into the darkness. *I'm coming Io. Do not be afraid.*

I open my eyes, the world is a grey blur. *I'm underwater.* I let out a stream of bubbles as I startle at this strange development. I kick up toward the surface. Lightning streaks across a stormy sky, illuminating my watery world. I propel myself upward, my lungs burn for air. My head breaks through the surface and I gulp down air. I take in my eerie surroundings. I am at the edge of a massive lake, I kick towards the shore and climb up the slippery bank. There is not a soul in sight. Red sand dunes extend in every direction and a snaking dirt road stretches to the horizon. I can make out a large city in the distance. Storm clouds boil in the sky while rolling thunder follows bright purple streaks of lightning.

I pass beneath a large tree with blood red flowers as I make my way down the hill top to the dirt road. There is no way to tell what hour of the day it might be. I break into a run. There is no time to lose. I need to find Io and get back to this lake. It must be a portal connecting the two worlds. I pray that going back is possible. I trust nothing that Terra has said. I ignore the vast desolate landscape as I run onward toward the City of the Dead.

PART II: THE MAGE

She wears strength
And darkness equally well,
The girl has always been
Half goddess, half hell.

-Nikita Gill

CHAPTER 16

"Sit up straight, Terra!"

"Yes, Mother," I mumble.

My Mother swats me with her needle work. I have the good sense not to flinch, that would merely earn me a harder crack. I have perfected a neutral mask to conceal my thoughts. When I was younger, my Mother would have beaten me for a mere eye roll or a scowl. I have learned how to please her.

"Your Father will be accompanying King

Eamon on his journey to Elaria. You will be going with him."

"Yes, Mother. I will start packing."

"Very good. Finish up here. I am meeting Lady Victoria for tea. When you are done, you may have personal time."

"Thank you, Mother."

My Mother sets down her sewing and gives me a quick peck on the cheek. I give her a light kiss on the cheek in return. This is the closest my Mother comes to affection. I suppose it is preferable to the rod. I remain silent as she dashes out the door with her skirts swishing behind her. Her handmaid hurries after her and I am alone at last. I stash my needle work in the chest beside my window. I grab my cloak from the wardrobe and head for the door.

I close my eyes as I exhale. *Free at last.* I smile to myself as I make my way down to the kitchens. I snag a butter roll from the basket on the wooden table. Lady Dana gives me a wink as I pass. I smile back, dodging the cooks as I dive out the back door to the gardens. I read into a run, kicking up pebbles as I go. I burst through the back gate and run through the tall grass. I slow as I near the sea cliff. I take a seat on my favorite rock. I breathe in the salt air as the waves crash against the rocks below, the sound and smell of the sea calms me. The sun glitters on the deep blue surface of the sea. No one expects anything of me out here. *Here, I am safe.*

I trace symbols in the air with my finger, golden light forms the runes that I have traced.

"Fleur."

The golden runes turn into pink wildflowers, I drop my hand and they fall all around me. *A girl should always give herself flowers.* I reach down to pick up a pristine pink daisy. I touch the soft petals, twirling the stem between my fingers. I tuck the stem behind my right ear. I gather up the fallen flowers and tie the bundle with a white ribbon from my skirt pocket.

"Nice trick."

I stiffen at the sound of his voice. *Kellan.* My heart begins to race, I force myself to take a soft calming breath and fix a smile to my face before I turn to face this vile man.

"Hello, Kellan," I say politely.

"Your Mother said I might find you here. It is time to prepare for our journey to Elaria. Might I help you with your belongings?"

"It is very kind of you to offer your help. I know how busy Father must be keeping you."

"I will always have time for my Beloved," he says, drawing near.

I fight the urge to take a step back. I take a step toward him instead. Kellan places a large calloused hand on my waist. I smile up at him. I learned the hard way that behaving any way other than a love struck fool will earn me a slap across the face or worse. I still have the scars to serve as a reminder.

"I knew you would warm up to me. I am a good man and together we will conquer the world."

"With you by my side, anything is possible," I say reverently, adding some shining tears to my eyes for the desired effect.

Kellan presses his hips to mine, I can feel his need digging into my stomach. I keep my mask firmly in place. I reward him with a sly smile. I reach down and stroke his crotch. Kellan closes his eyes, his lips part ever so slightly. *An act of self preservation that should earn his trust. This great oaf. I will relish the moment I drive my sword through his black heart. Patience, dear heart. The moment is almost at hand.*

"Come. We best get back before I ravage you."

"Surely, you can spare a moment," I say pulling on his belt.

I take a step back and turn around. Kellan lets out a ragged exhale. He runs his hand down my spine, loosening the laces of my bodice. I close my eyes as the fabric of my dress falls away. Kellan gently turns me to face him. I carefully undo his belt, setting it down on the grass. I slip my hands into the waist band of his pants and pull them down slowly. Kellan pulls his shirt over his head, revealing his impressive physique. *Perhaps I should keep him around. I may need a distraction from time to time.*

Kellan lifts me off my feet and sets me down in the grass. I gaze up at him with lust and longing. His eyes rake over my flesh, his hands exploring. I close my eyes as he lowers himself onto me. A soft cry escapes me as he invades me. *Someday I will be with a man who loves and cares for my soul. Someday I will be more than a lovely face with no name and no voice.*

CHAPTER 17

I neatly fold some traveling clothes for the road. I place them in my pack along with a few tinctures and balms, my favorite necklace, and a few provisions I pilfered from the kitchens. I plop down on the floor to sharpen my sword and daggers, this small mundane act calms me. I was able to lose Kellan after our cliff side encounter.

My body aches. I scrubbed my skin raw in the tub afterwards. My maid, Elsie brought me my tea. *No babe for me. I'd rather be flayed alive than give that bastard a child.* Kellan is my

Father's right hand man. He is twenty eight, ten years my senior. Kellan saved my Father's life on the battle field. My Father, generous man he is, promised Kellan his daughter's hand. I was sixteen years old at the time, Kellan was twenty six. Kellan agreed to wait until my eighteenth birthday to wed. I turned eighteen three days ago. Kellan agreed to wait for marriage, he has been visiting my bed since the marriage was arranged. I am no virgin bride. I suppose being spoiled by the man who will be my future husband makes no difference. *Having a say in the matter would have been greatly appreciated.*

Mother loves Kellan, she thinks a strong, handsome warrior such as he will be a fine husband who will sire strong sons and lovely daughters. My Father being a hard man, Mother dare not hope for a tender, kind man who would hold me through the storm or treat me with respect. My Mother was never granted such a kindness. Why should her daughter receive such treatment? Mother always says, 'We are women. We were fashioned to endure, to survive the cruelty of men. Do not long for true love, Terra. It does not exist.'

My Mother taught me long ago not to cry in my Father's presence. 'Tears are not your weapon. The only weapon you possess is the one between your legs.' My Mother was not my Father's first choice. Mother was given to my Father after his true betrothed fled with her lover, *Brigid Flynn, heir to the throne of Caelen.* It was quite the scandal. Crowned Princess spurns the Lord Commander and marries her Knight in secret. My Mother tried her best to be a dutiful, loyal wife. She took all her beatings without shedding a single tear. I always admired her for that. I would pretend to be asleep when she would come into my bedroom to check on me. That is the only time she would lower her walls to cry, in the darkness when she thought no one would betray her weakness. My Mother lives a half life, serving an abusive man who has no love for her. I am no product of love, merely a child sired out of duty.

I always hated the idea of Princess Brigid Flynn and her lover. The child that they conceived in love. Another Princess who knows nothing of pain and sorrow. My rage simmers like the tiny flames rising from glowing embers of a fire not yet brought to life. *One day, I will make them all pay. I will suffer in silence no more. One day, I will sit the throne and no one will ever hurt me again.*

I jump as a knock at my door rings through my chamber. "Come in!"

"Almost finished?" My Father asks.

"Yes, Father. I am ready to depart."

"Very good. Let's head to the stables. It is time."

I take one last look around my room, I will miss my bed. I sigh as I hurriedly gather my things. I extinguish the fire in my hearth and stride after my Father. Our Lord Commander is dressed in his best, deerskin pants, cotton under shirt, chainmail, and a leather jerkin. A gold arm band glitters on his left bicep. Leather gloves are tucked into his heavy leather sword belt, his long sword has been freshly sharpened and polished. His favorite dagger is on his right hip, I can see the serpent etched onto the silver hilt. The serpent is the sigil of House Kade.

I follow my Father through the corridor in silence. He is not one for idle chatter. My Father believes that women should only spoke when spoken to, a lesson I learned at an early age when he struck my Mother for speaking back to him in front of another warrior. She had a black eye for a week. I got a salve from Selene to help heal her swollen eye.

When we reach the stables, I excuse myself to ready my horse. My Father nods and I find my noble steed, Ares in his stall. Ares is a striking black stallion with a glossy man and tail. He moves like a shadow, a stealthy mount with stamina to match his impressive speed. Kellan gave him to me as an engagement present. *Probably the only proper gift that man will ever bestow upon me.*

I stroke Ares' nose as I feed him a carrot from my pack. I press my forehead against his. "Ready for another adventure?"

Ares nuzzles my hand and gives a gentle snort. "I thought so," I say with a small smile.

I brush his back and give him a loving pat before laying his blanket on him. I hoist my saddle up onto his back. Ares stands still as I secure all the belts and buckles. When everything is to my satisfaction, I swing up into the saddle and nudge him with the heels of my boots. Ares trots forward into the morning light.

Across the yard I spot Rowan speaking to his Mother, Selene. I have always thought him handsome. We played together as children. I always hoped he would court me when we were older. Fate decided that we would never be. Everyone knows that I have been promised to Kellan, a warrior no one would dare cross. Kellan's temper is known far and wide. I shake my head and turn away. *Such a thing will never be. It is probably for the best. I would not know real love if it hit me in the face.*

"Watch out!"

I narrowly avoid an arrow that wizzes past my left ear. I jerk Ares' reins and he rears up in alarm. A harried warrior with wild black curls comes sprinting toward me.

"You almost rode right through the archery range! Are you alright?"

"It seems you spared me from a rather gruesome fate," I say sarcastically.

My valiant hero watches me with the keen green eyes and offers me a gorgeous smile. My heart skips a beat. I swallow and feel my cheeks flush.

"What's your name?"

"You must be new," I say rolling my eyes. "I am Terra Kade."

"Ah the Lord Commander's daughter. My deepest apologies, my Lady. May I escort you to the front line?"

"That won't be necessary, Sir. Watch your aim," I say giving him a mischievous wink.

"Don't you want to know my name?" He asks tilting his painfully beautiful face to the side.

"I can't see how that would change anything," I say with a sad smile.

My hero frowns at my expression. I see a flicker of concern in his eyes. *Leave you idiot, before Kellan spots you with him.* I give him a nod as I give Ares a sharp kick. Ares carries me away. I do not allow myself to look back. It is for the best. He is a good man. *I am nothing but, trouble. If he does not have the good sense to stay away, I will save him from me and all the pain that being with me would bring.*

CHAPTER 18

We make camp several hours after crossing the border into Elaria, a quiet grove among the oak trees, a rushing river just beyond. I set up my tent and stash my pack before heading to the cook tent. I am greeted by the smell of fresh baked flat bread, eggs, fresh oranges, and crispy bacon. I take a deep inhale. *Bless you, Finn.*

I stand in line behind a group of cajoling warriors slapping each other on the back. I keep to myself most of the time. My 'friends,' Fiona and Shannon, are empty headed, twits.

My Mother insisted that I keep companions. I tolerate the likes of them to keep my Mother off my back, a rather draining chore. *A rather lonely existence.*

The line moves quickly, I reach the front and Finn offers me a loaded plate. "Thank you, Finn."

"Of course, my Lady," Finn replies with a small smile.

I carry my plate over to a large log by the fire. Several groups of warriors, washer women, cook staff, and healers are taking their meals together. I am not in the mood for forced pleasantries, so I sit alone. I prefer to eat in silence anyway. The fire feels good, the sun has sunk behind the mountains and the air is chill. I spoon some scrambled eggs onto my buttered flatbread. I peel a large orange and tear a section free. The sweet tangy juice is a treat. Fruit is my favorite.

I spy Rowan and his friend Bran sitting together, talking about the *Princess,* no doubt. I roll my eyes and turn to my right, just in time to see Fiona and Shannon approaching. I let out a pained sigh of frustration. *So much for peace and quiet.* I plaster a smile on and use my sweetest voice.

"There you two are," I say tossing my blonde hair. "I was wondering where you had gone."

"We got stuck with kitchen duty," Fiona says with a scowl.

"Where have you been?" Shannon asks, eyeing me.

"Just set up my tent and came over for dinner."

"Lucky," Fiona says with a huff, plopping down with her dinner plate.

"Saw your friend over near the healers's tent."

"Hmmmm," I grunt around a mouthful of eggs and bacon.

"You going to let her get away with that?" Shannon hisses.

"That is the least of my worries," I mutter to the ground.

"What was that?" Fiona asks half heartedly.

I wave her question away, "Nothing."

"Have you heard about the plan for Castle Greenwood?" Shannon asks.

"I am the Lord Commander's daughter."

"No need to be cheeky, love," Fiona teases.

"We're meant to help secure the border once the first wave breaches the castle walls."

"Sounds like a good time," I say sarcastically.

"You should learn your place. Your Father will be counting on you," Fiona says sternly.

I bite my tongue as I rise to clean my plate at the wash basin. I stalk off without a backward glance. *I have no patience for this farce today. I'm going rogue.* I wash the remnants of my meal from the green ceramic plate. I set it in the rack to dry. I bump into a tall someone as I turn back to the sink.

"I beg your pardon. Ah, we meet again Lady Terra."

I look up into the green eyes of the handsome archer with the black curls. Time stand still as I force my tongue to form words.

"Hello again," I manage with an ill concealed blush.

"Would you like to know my name yet?"

"You do seem rather eager for me to hear it. Pray tell," I say with a grin.

"I am Xavier Fen of Caelen, my Lady. Pleased to properly make your acquaintance."

"Well met, Sir Xavier of House Fen."

Xavier bows deeply, as he rises he brushes his lips against the top of my right hand. The chivalrous gesture sets my heart racing. I am not sure how to react. *My gut instinct is telling me to run. There is no such thing as love. This is all an act.* I desperately wish this could be my happy ending, my way out. I gently withdraw my hand and turn to leave.

"I'll see you on the road," Xavier says.

Not wanting to give him false hope, I merely nod before I walk away. Xavier watches me go, I feel his eyes on my back as I put distance between us. *This is for the best.*

Kellan would not be pleased. This is for Xavier's own good. I am nothing but, trouble.

I break down my tent and pack it away in my saddle bag. I lead Ares over to the river bank for a nice long drink of water. I fill three water skins and tie them to the back of my saddle. My mind has been a jumble of thoughts, I am eager to get on the road and silence them all for a while. Riding calms me. I walk Ares back to the column of mounted warriors. I haul myself up into the saddle. I stroke Ares's neck lovingly as we move out. We continue our march to the east into the heart of Elaria. I have a terrible feeling. My stomach churns, I feel bile rising in my throat. *Something will be set in motion today. There is no turning back now.*

CHAPTER 19

I lie in wait for the signal. I can just make out the archers perched high up in the trees ahead. I see Gwen loose an arrow, it sails through the air and finds it's target with a sickening thud. The sentry falls from the wall without a sound. His companion turns and takes an arrow to the chest, he stumbles on valiantly to the pyre, snatches a torch from a sconce and drops it onto the pitch. Shouts ring out and the signal fires along the wall blaze to life. *They know we are here.*

Our first wave crashes through the underbrush, sprinting toward the castle walls. Archers appear on the walls, arrows rain down, many warriors succumb to the fatal fallout. I grip my sword so tight that I feel the pommel dig into my palm. The pain helps me focus. *Do not hesitate. Keep moving. A delay may send you into Death's embrace. Strike first, make it count.*

Warriors are rising all around me, I can hear my Father, delivering some earth shattering speech. A roar rises up from the ranks and suddenly we are running. I am lost to the Chaos. Death is all around me, as well as the desperate fight for life. I often feel that I lose myself on the battlefield. It feels as though I am watching from above. I slash my sword and am rewarded with hot arterial spray, my victim drops to his knees, he never saw me coming, a kind end in a cruel world. My muscles burn as I run through the motions. Slash, parry, stab, *kill.* My Father made sure I was as fierce as any son of Caelen, with the cunning to match. At least I can say I made him proud. I may not have earned his love but, I dare say I earned his respect.

We have breeched the castle walls. I follow the surge of black clad warriors into the castle grounds. Servants flee in terror, abandoning their good King and Queen. The great doors to the throne room have been thrown open. Thieves are dashing down the stairs with all manner of gold, jewels, and coin, whatever they can carry away swiftly. Several raiders have begun to fight among themselves, I slip by them and search for the royal chambers. My Father instructed us to secure them royal family, no one of royal blood is to come to harm.

I find a few Ladies of the Court hiding in the spinning room behind their looms and spinning wheels. They shriek and cower at the sight of me, soaked from head to toe in the blood of their kin. I leave them and continue my search. I find the King's chambers, looted and abandoned. The Queen's chambers is in the same state of disarray. When I come across the Princess's chambers, I pause, the corner of the rug in front on the hearth has been over turned. I pull back the rug to find a trap door. I climb down into an earthen passageway, quietly closing the door over head. I follow the dimly lit passage for a time and emerge into a large under ground cavern. I see daylight ahead, there is a tunnel that leads out into the open. I head toward the light, crouching low.

I squint as I shield my eyes from the light of day. I can hear birdsong and the rustling of wind in the leaves. A scream of agony, freezes me in place. I turn my face toward the direction of the scream. There just through the trees, I can see a girl of my age, pinned to the ground by a particularly vile man, one of my Father's friends, Uther. He is a well known rapist and scoundrel, no stranger to violence against women. My heart twists at the sight. The girl is no match for his size and brute strength, Uther backhands her across the face, she crashes to the ground in a heap, she lies still and I fear the worst. I creep towards them, staying low and silent. I manage to get within earshot, concealing myself behind a blackberry bush. I raise my sword and nearly drop it in fear when Uther lets out a blood curdling scream of his own. *That's it, girl. End him.*

I peer through the foliage, my mouth falls open as I take it all in. The girl presses her small hands to Uther's face which is *melting beneath her touch.* Her hands glow like burning embers, small blue flames licking her slender fingers. The flesh of her hands and forearms blackening and burning away to reveal obsidian scales, shimmering in the sunlight. *A Shapeshifter? Impossible.*

Uther falls backward as the girl shovers him off with all her might. She stares at his mangled, melted face in horror before taking off through the trees. I stare after her, awe struck. I jog after her, keeping a distance, I'd like to keep my face. I watch from behind an ancient Ash tree as she collides with Rowan. I feel a sting of jealousy as her tenderly scoops her into his muscular arms, cradling her close, her head rests against the hard plane of his chest. I can see her shoulders trembling as she sobs silently.

Selene helps Rowan settle the girl in the healer's cart. I watch Rowan as he gazes at her trembling form. *He is lost. Completely spell-bound by this little thing.* I sigh. *Love all around but, not a drop for me.* I turn away from the sickening sight. I shake my head to clear it of my self pity. There is no time for such weakness. I stride back to the castle. I freeze when I spot a form lying on the forest floor. A maiden, the *Princess Mara.* A deep stab wound in her chest has stained her lovely gown crimson, a pool of blood has matted her auburn hair, her countenance is full of dewy youth. *A Beauty, what a waste of life. Freya call her home.*

I set off to find my Father to report the Princess's death, King Eamon will be furious, our orders were to detain the royal family. No member of House Everwood was to come to harm. I close my eyes, the Princess's pale face swims before me. I imagine her in life, laughing, dancing, and running through the trees with her hand maids. *Rest well, Princess.*

PART III: BEYOND THE VEIL

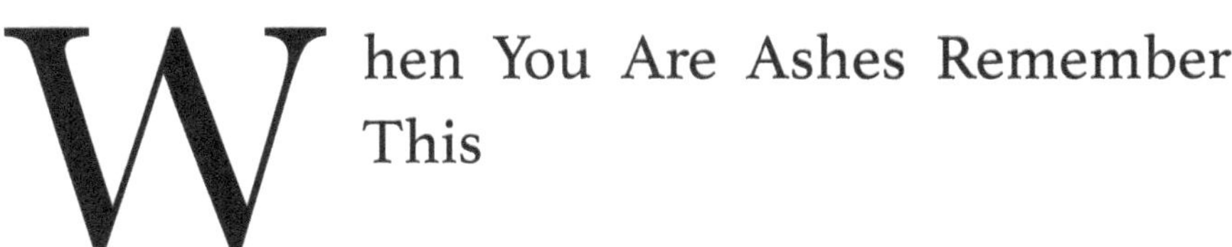

When You Are Ashes Remember This

THEY WILL INSULT YOU,
Hurt you,
Defeat you,
Betray you,
Injure you,
Set you aflame
And watch

You burn.

But they
Will not,
Shall not,
Cannot
Destroy you.

Because you,
Like Rome
Were built on ashes,
And you,
Like a *phoenix*
Know how to
Rise
And
Resurrect.

- *Nikita Gill*

CHAPTER 20

IO

Time has no meaning here. Thick grey clouds churn in a midnight sky, several stars beckon to me as I gaze upward. We have been walking for what feels like hours. Our tempers are short and the road stretches out before us. The City of the Dead looms ahead, I start to run.

"What are you doing?" Terra calls after me, the exasperation in her voice evident.

"Trying to get there faster," I huff between breaths.

"Suit yourself," Terra sighs, slightly increasing her ambling pace.

I break into a quick stride, feeling the wind drag her fingers through my hair. *I'm coming, Rowan. We'll be home soon.* Terra appears beside me, causing me to jump.

"Jeez, what the hell!" I shout in alarm.

"Sorry," Terra mutters with a snicker. "Just trying to keep up."

"Next time announce yourself. Maybe a small cough, clear of the throat," I suggest with an eye roll.

"Noted," Terra says, the corner of her lips twitch upward ever so slightly, such a minute movement, I wonder if I imagined it.

We move at a brisk pace down the dirt road. The City grows larger with every footfall. I dare to hope that we will rescue our loved ones and escape this place. A sudden thought seizes me.

"Can we find anyone we've lost here?"

Terra regards me with knowing eyes. "Your Father is not here, Io."

"How can you possibly know that?" I ask defensively, annoyed that she read my thoughts.

"Because I have wandered this realm before. I have never seen Connor Erikson on this plane."

"Why isn't he here?"

"There are a few explanations for his absence. He may be in another dimension. He may be trapped between our world and the Underworld, bound as a wandering soul with unfinished business. Or...". Terra pauses.

"Or what?"

"He may still be alive."

"That's not possible. My Mother said he died in her arms." I insist.

"Mothers lie." Terra says grimly.

Her words hang in the space between us and I run onward. Drowning out my doubts with pounding steps and deep cleansing breaths. The landscape changes drastically as we pass into the shadow of the city walls. The red sands and dusty dirt road give way to dark soil and a blanket of thick green grass. The towering walls that surround the city are carved from volcanic rock. Frightful creatures have been carved into the surface, demons, dragons, serpents, a massive three headed dog, cats, ravens, and Gods and Goddesses of Death. It is a dark, terrible beauty. I am drawn to the ornate gate of polished obsidian and tourmaline, strange runes and symbols are embossed in gold. As we approach the gates creak on massive iron hinges as they permit us entry. I gasp as I get my first glimpse of the City of the Dead. My eyes take in an explosion of color that I was not expecting. The shop fronts, houses, and rows of vendors at a street market are dripping in vibrant hues. My eyes roam over the delightful display. And the people, are not specters, ghouls, or the souls of the damned, they look like living people, no evidence of their death at all.

"Weird, huh?"

"Definitely not what I expected," I say,

trailing off as I get distracted by a woman in a silk white gown, approaching from our right.

"Terra, what a pleasure to see you again, my dear," the woman says with a smile.

"Lady Snow, you are looking as lovely as ever," Terra says with genuine affection.

I raise my eyebrows at the exchange. Terra reads my expression and indulges my curiosity.

"Lady Snow, this is Princess Io Flynn of Caelen," Terra says by way of introduction.

"Your Grace, my condolences," Lady Snow says with a bow of her head.

"Thank you," I say awkwardly bowing in return.

"Um, where to now?" I ask, scanning the city square for a clue as to where I might find Rowan.

"Follow me," Terra says with a wave of her arm. "Until we meet again, old friend," Terra says with a nod to Lady Snow.

"Good luck, Ladies," Lady Snow says before disappearing into the teeming crowd.

"Was she offering condolences for my death?"

"That is pretty standard upon arrival," Terra replies.

I follow Terra through several narrow alley ways and winding streets that pass beneath towering homes and shops. The cobble stone streets are neatly swept, no foul puddles of muck or horse droppings in sight. Our footsteps echo through the empty streets. Everyone must be at the market. *Where are we headed? Is this some kind of trap?*

"Where are we-?"

"Shhhh," Terra hisses.

I scowl but, hold my tongue as she ushers me up a flight of stairs under a bright blue archway painted with orange marigolds. We wind our way up to a dizzying height, we finally reach a small landing that opens up into a large observatory. A fire is roaring in the enormous hearth. Plush purple carpets cover the stone floor. A woman is standing at the archway leading out to a lavish balcony over looking the city.

"Come in my, darlings," the woman says as she turns to face us.

I realize she must be related to Terra, they have the same icy blue eyes and long blonde hair. Her face glows with vitality and youth. She smiles at me with knowing eyes. I shift uneasily under her penetrating gaze.

"Welcome, Io. I am Freya," the woman says gently.

Her skin is smooth and fair, not a single line or blemish. She is ageless, a flawless Goddess. She wears a cream colored gown and a dark green cloak, trimmed with wolf fur. A golden cuff gleams on her left wrist, a gold talisman at her throat is etched with wildflowers. She has a calm demeanor. I feel at ease in her presence.

"Are you a Goddess?"

"When it suits me," Freya replies with a wink.

I smile despite myself. Goddess or not, we

can use all the help we can get. Freya draws a small glass vial from her pocket, I can see a silver liquid shimmering inside. She offers the vial to me. I take it from her outstretched hand, examining it closely.

"This tincture will heal the sick and injured. Even if the drinker is a mere breath away from death."

"Thank you," I say looking up to meet Freya's eyes. I startle when I stare into the empty space where she stood a moment ago.

Terra laughs at my bewildered expression and claps a hand on my back. "You'll get used to it."

Terra walks out onto the terrace over looking the city streets. She closes her eyes and rests her palms on the stone banister. I wait patiently as Terra meditates. I slide quietly to the floor and lean my head against the stone archway, my eyes close of their own accord and I drift off.

"I've got him!"

I jerk awake, knocking my head on the

stone archway. I wince as I rub the back of my head and rise. "Who?" I ask in a groggy voice.

"Your Hero of course," Terra says.

"What about your friend?"

"I found him too. Let's get moving."

Terra grabs her cloak from a chair by the hearth. The fire has burned down considerably, I worry that we have little time left. Terra sets a quick pace. I stay right on her heels. We descend the spiral staircase and burst out into the streets. There are still people wandering about the market. Shops have lit their lamps and delicious smells tempt me as we run past several restaurants. I try to memorize our route but, lose track after several sharp turns and passageways. Anxiety gnaws at me as we move deeper into the city. Terra comes to an abrupt stop in an open square, I have to hop to my left to avoid crashing into her. A large stone castle casts a dark shadow over the square, several torches lining a staircase roar to life of their own accord as Terra approaches the steep stone steps.

"That's not creepy," I mutter as I fall in step behind Terra.

"You'll get used to the creep factor too," Terra says over her shoulder.

Terra and I are drenched in sweat by the time we reach the massive double doors at the top of the stairs. A great brass knocker shaped as the head of a lion is positioned in the center of the right door. Terra knocks three times, three deep booms echo within. The door slowly opens and a tall muscular dark skinned man in a deep blue robe answers.

"May I help you?" He asks looking down his long nose at the pair of us.

"We've come to see your Mistress," Terra says.

"Who shall I say has come to call?"

"Terra Kade and Io Flynn."

The man retreats inside, he returns after a moment, holding the door wide to permit us entry. "Follow me."

The entrance hall is exquisite, black marble floors and immense stone columns that disappear high above our heads to support the vaulted ceiling, floating twinkling lights mimic the stars in the night sky. Our escort leads us down a walkway that opens up into a splendid garden full of lush greenery and exotic flowers. There is a pond in the center with a flowing fountain, a statue of three women standing together, each holding a torch in one hand. Beyond the garden we pass beneath a grand stone archway covered in ivy and white roses. We step into a grand hall that is decorated with large urns holding all sorts of plants with beautiful blooms or succulent fruits. The floor is made up of large stone slabs, the spaces between have been filled with water. Some of the larger gaps have water lilies and small fishes swimming just beneath the surface. On the far side of the room is a large red sofa covered in tasseled throw pillows, among them sits a beautiful woman with ivory skin, long flowing brown hair, and sharp golden eyes.

We step carefully across the stones to reach

our gracious host. She watches us patiently as we approach. She is dressed in a flowing black gown that hugs her curves and reveals an ample bosom. I look to Terra for an indication of a proper greeting. Terra drops to one knee and bows her head. I follow suit and wait.

"Hekate, Goddess of the Heavens, Earth, and Underworld, please hear our prayer."

"Rise, my daughters. What is it you seek?"

I stand when Terra does, turning my eyes to the Goddess.

"We have lost loved ones. We have come to guide them back to the land of the living," Terra says with strength and conviction.

"You have risked much to come here, Terra Kade," Hekate says, rising from her comfortable perch.

She seems to glide toward us, rather than walk. She is tall, her figure lithe but, strong. Her countenance is breathtaking, her beauty demands attention. I have a strange feeling that she possesses great power, I can feel the hum of energy radiating from her, like crackling lightning before a storm. Her movements are fluid, her manner provocative. She seems the type who would lure a man to his death and drink his blood.

"You have nothing to fear from me, Io Flynn," Hekate says, turning to me without warning. "You have a great destiny laid out before you. You will leave the Underworld unscathed."

"I'm not so sure about a great destiny. I will be leaving though."

Hekate smiles as she regards me with those luminous golden eyes. "You have only just set foot on the path. Stay the course."

"Goddess Hekate, I believe you may know where we can find the men we seek," Terra says.

So Terra is looking for a man as well. Who could he be? Hekate considers Terra for a moment before walking over to a table I did not notice before. She opens a small wooden box and pulls out a large ornate key. She offers it to Terra who takes it without question.

"This key will open the door in the next room. You will find the men you seek within. A word of caution, not all is as it seems in the realm of lost souls. You will face demons who will try to stop you from reuniting, they do not like to surrender the souls they have claimed. Take torches to help light your way. The fire repels demons and will help you find your way out."

"Thank you, Goddess Hekate," Terra says with a deep bow. I bow to the Goddess as well.

"Good luck, Wayfinders," Hekate says, stepping aside so that we may pass.

We walk to the archway beside Hekate's sofa. Terra stops to lift a blazing torch from the wall sconce. I take the one on the opposite side of the archway. Terra and I meet eyes, I nod and we step through the archway. The next room is small, stone floor and two long windows on opposite walls showing a deep blue sky with endless stars. In front of us, a large white door with large brass handles and an ornate key hole that matches Hekate's key. The crackling of our torches is the only sound in the room.

"Ready?" Terra asks, glancing at me with fearful eyes.

"Let's go find the way," I say, trying to keep my voice from shaking.

Terra nods and grips the key tightly. I realize that the air feels much cooler at the door. A shiver runs down my spine and I draw my cloak closer around me. I wish I had some kind of weapon.

"Here," Terra says offering me a knife from her belt.

"Thank you," I say with a grimace. "Let's get this over with."

Terra pushes the key into the lock and turns. A metallic click sounds as we each push on the brass door handles. I swallow my fear and grip my knife. A dim light shines through the widening opening. We step through together and find ourselves in a forest at dawn.

Not a soul to be seen. I hear birdsong and the rustling of an early morning breeze through the trees.

"Don't be fooled, keep your guard up," Terra whispers.

I nod silently as the blood pounds in my ears. I slowly scan our surroundings as we move deeper into the forest. The doors thud shut behind us and we both jump in alarm. I try to memorize the look of the doors and this section of the woods. This might be our only way back. We walk in silence, listening hard for the slightest sound that could warn us of unforeseen danger. The tree line starts to thicken, casting long shadows. Terra grips my forearm and I freeze immediately, she points ahead just to the right. I follow her finger and my breath catches, a pair of eyes stares back at me through the foliage.

CHAPTER 21

ROWAN

I catch my breath as the vast obsidian doors creak open. *Io's here, I just know it in my heart.* I step into the city square and take in the riot of color. *Not what I expected...and the people, are actual people. No moaning ghouls, ghosts dragging chains, or undead.* Everyone is milling about purchasing fresh fruits, vegetables, cuts of meat, plates of food, and freshly baked breads and sweets. There are even children running through the streets, laughing and playing. *How odd. I was expecting more of a hell scape. Maybe some monsters and cursed souls?*

I make my way through the market. I wonder if Io spoke to anyone here? I get the sense that I am being watched. I turn to my right to see a beautiful woman dressed in a white gown, smiling at me warmly. I approach her.

"I beg your pardon, my Lady, have you seen a young woman pass by? She has warm brown skin, brown eyes, and long black hair. She was wearing a dark green gown," I say, searching her eyes for any flicker of recognition.

"I may have," the woman says. "Who is this girl to you?"

"I am her guard. She is my friend as well."

"Seems as though you have failed her, if this is where your search has led you."

"I am trying to remedy that," I say, my impatience starting to grow.

"So you are," the woman says, regarding me with dark blue eyes. "She came this way, your maiden. She is in the company of a friend of mine."

"And who might this friend be?"

"Terra Kade."

"Thank you. Lady?"

"Lady Snow. Hurry now, you must get back to the door. Terra and Io went to Hekate's Tower. Follow that street and take the third alley on the left, all the way to the end. It is the tallest tower."

I bow to Lady Snow and take off. I dodge a group of ladies carrying baskets of ruby red pomegranates. A group of children, kicking a ball, scurry as I come tearing through the alley. An enormous stone tower blocks out the sky ahead. I find a large set of doors with a lion's head knocker at the top of a mountain of stairs. I slam the brass ring down on the lion's nose. The door opens and a large dark skinned man in a midnight blue robe glares at me with a harassed expression.

"What in the seven hells can I do for you?" He drawls, looking me over.

"Terra Kade. Is she here? I am looking for the woman she is traveling with, I was told by Lady Snow that I would find them in this tower."

"Come with me," the man sighs deeply.

"Thank you," I pant as I cross the threshold.

The cavernous room is dripping in splendor, black tourmaline and obsidian walls, immense columns that disappear into the darkness of the vaulted ceiling high over head. The ceiling itself is a living night sky, complete with glittering constellations and shooting stars. The floor is black marble with veins of gold. We pass through the entry hall into a splendid garden. The floor is a waterway dotted with large, lava rock stepping stones. Exotic plants flourish, blooming in every imaginable hue and filling the air with heady scents. At the heart of the garden there is a grand fountain that has a triple Goddess statue in its center, honoring the *Maiden, Mother, and Crone.* Each Goddess holds a torch high with her right hand. *Hekate.*

We pass the magnificent fountain and I see the Goddess herself, perched on a plush red sofa, piled high with tasseled cushions. She locks eyes with me and stands in alarm. I feel dread pooling in my belly. *Something is wrong. Where are Io and Terra?*

"You are supposed to be in the realm of Lost Souls," Hekate says, as though I know what the hell she is babbling about.

"Sorry to disappoint. Terra did not arm me with a map," I retort.

"Charming," Hekate says. "I see why she likes you."

"Where is Io?"

"Terra is looking for her lover in the realm of Lost Souls."

"That sounds fun. Can't wait to join the party."

"I will show you the way."

Hekate sweeps past me, gossamer gown trailing in her wake. I follow her quick stride back through the garden. She walks through an archway I did not notice on our way in. We step into a small room with tall windows on either wall and white double doors with large brass handles and a key hole. Hekate steps forward and places her hands on the door. She whispers, "Arawn, God of Death, grant me passage."

The white doors open wide, an eerie white light spills into the dark room. Hekate beckons me forward. I step forward and face the open door. There is a forest at twilight within, tendrils of mist reach toward us and a cold wind rustles the leaves of the ancient trees.

"You will find your love within," Hekate says holding her right arm out toward the forest.

"Thank you, Goddess Hekate," I say with a bow.

"Good luck, Rowan of Caelen."

I turn away from the Goddess and step into the woods. I keep walking when I hear the doors close behind me. I keep moving, listening, scanning the trees for any sign of life. The further I walk, the darker the shadows, the quiet is suffocating. I draw my sword, to keep my mind at ease. I spot some boot tracks in the muddy soil beneath an Ash tree. Two sets of tracks. I follow them for a time, scarcely looking up. They suddenly stop at a clearing. The clearing is covered with a blanket of fallen leaves but, they look undisturbed. *Where did you go?*

A sudden whistling sound sends me crashing to the ground. A loud thud confirms my suspicion, I look up to find an arrow with bright green fletching sunk into the bark of the oak tree at my back. I scan the tree line on the opposite side of the clearing. *There you are.* A cloaked figure with a hood pulled down low, perches on the limb of a tall pine. I look for any friends. *Two more perched in neighboring pines. A group of four, spread out in the underbrush below.*

I slip my own bow from my shoulder and

quickly snatch an arrow from my quiver. I loose an arrow at the first archer. He falls without a sound, landing with a sickening crunch on one of the men below, neither rises. The two remaining archers shout in alarm and fumble with their quivers. I fire two arrows in rapid succession. Two archers fall to their kinsman below. The three remaining on the ground sprint toward me. I stop two in their tracks with arrows. The final survivor rushes onward. I meet him in the clearing, easily deflecting his first swing. He kicks at my right foot, knocking me off balance. My attacker advances and stabs at my torso. I narrowly avoid the thrust. I spring back and kick him in his belly. He falls back and his hood slips down.

My attacker rises. A beautiful *woman* with silver hair and turquoise eyes. Tall and lean, with a vicious streak. I freeze in a crouch. She regards me with those blazing turquoise eyes, her breath coming in short gasps.

"Who are you?" I demand, keeping my sword at the ready.

"I will ask the same of you," She says, never taking her eyes off me.

"I am Rowan McGlaughlin of Caelen. I am looking for Io Flynn. The Goddess Hekate told me that Io and Terra came into this realm."

"I saw them. Our scouts took them to the village."

"Take me to them," I growl.

"You killed my people. I will do no such thing!"

"I will not ask a second time."

"You would kill a woman?"

"With a sword in hand? Yes."

The warrior scoffs and regards me with narrowed eyes. She steps to her left. I shift to my left, careful to keep her in my sight. I grip my sword. She keeps a tight grip on her own.

"I don't have all god damn night."

"Time has no meaning here. This is the

realm of Lost Souls. No one leaves once they enter this forest."

"We'll be the first ones."

"So sure of yourself, Rowan McGlaughlin of Caelen? You will need that fire to survive this place."

The female warrior returns her sword to its scabbard. I sheath my own blade. The woman extends her right hand.

"I am Wren."

I take her hand and give it a firm grip. "Pleased to meet you, Wren. Shall we?"

Wren nods and turns back toward the trees. We walk in silence for a time. I study our surroundings. I draw my dagger from my hip, I mark trees with a big 'x.' *This should help us find our way back.*

"She must be the love of your life. A man would not go beyond the veil for just any woman."

"She is indeed. A truly extraordinary woman."

"She is lucky to have your love. We are

nearly there."

The trees have begun to thin. I can see grasslands up ahead. Tendrils of smoke are rising up from a valley below. We come to the ridge over looking the valley. A switch back dirt trail leads down to the valley floor where a sprawling village teems with life. Homes of stone with wood and thatch roof tops cover most of the valley. A crystal clear river runs through the center of the valley. Plots of land have been cleared for agriculture. Horses and cows graze in green pastures, children run through the fields laughing and hollering.

"Welcome to the Valley of Bones."

"Inviting name," I mutter.

"We don't get many guests," Wren says shrugging.

We begin our descent to the valley floor. The steep trail keeps me on my toes. Wren moves swiftly, hopping from rock to rock and jogging along the smoother stretches of path. Sweat drips down my face as I match Wren's pace. I focus on my feet, not wanting to trip and topple off the cliff face. Wren pauses for a brief moment to listen. I glance to my right and realize that we are more than half way down the trail. I can hear voices, music, and smell a delicious stew from the cook fires.

"Terra and Io would have been taken to the High Priestess. We'll head there first."

I nod and we push onward. My legs are burning by the time we reach the end of the trail. I stand tall and keep my face neutral.

"The trail is fierce," Wren says with a slight smile.

"Piece of cake," I say with a wave of my hand.

Wren rolls her eyes and walks on toward the village. *For fuck sake!* I hobble after her, every muscle screaming with each step. A swarm of children descend on Wren as she sets foot in the village. I smile at the cacophony of excited voices and smiling faces. Wren scoops up a little girl with blonde braids. The girl can be no more than four, she nuzzles Wren's cheek and hugs her close. They have the same turquoise eyes.

A little boy notices me hanging back. He stares at me, tilting his head to one side as though he is not quite sure what to make of me.

"Who is he?" The boy asks, pointing at me.

Every child turns to gape at me in unison. Wren walks over to me. The children flock after her. They circle me, poking and prodding as though I am a prized cow.

"This is Rowan McGlaughlin of Caelen. He is looking for his travel companions, two women. The scouts brought them to the village earlier. Can you tell us where they were taken?"

"They are with the High Priestess," a little girl with chestnut brown curls squeaks.

"Thank you, Maddie," Wren says, gently patting her small shoulder.

Wren bids the children farewell. We walk deeper into the village. It seems like everyone is either preparing or enjoying the evening meal. My stomach rumbles, my mouth waters as we pass the bonfires where the villagers are taking their meals. We come to the end of the houses. Wren leads me through a field of wildflowers. Fireflies take flight as we wade through the tall grass. There is a large stone temple up ahead. Blazing torches line a pathway to the doors. Wren pulls the right door open wide and steps inside. I cross the threshold and find myself in a haze of incense. It takes a moment for my eyes to adjust to the dim light.

On the far end of the room, a grand altar is lit by hundreds of candles. A tall woman in a white linen dress is lighting a bundle of dried sage. She turns at the sound of our footsteps. She assesses me with curious violet eyes, her face is narrow, the nose long and slightly upturned, her black hair is long and loose. She offers Wren a loving smile.

"Who have you brought to me, Wren?"

"High Priestess, this is Rowan Mc-

Glaughlin of Caelen. He is searching for his travel companions. Our scouts found them in the woods."

"Right this way," the High Priestess says, holding her right arm out.

Wren and I follow her down a short hallway to a room filled with cots before a crackling hearth. Sitting on a cot before the fire is my Io. Terra is pacing back and forth in an agitated manner. She spots us first. Io looks up to see why Terra has stopped pacing. When she sees me she rises slowly. I take a step toward her and she runs at me. Io launches herself into my arms and I catch her, hugging her close. I bury my face in her hair, breathing in her familiar smell.

"Is it really you?"

"In the flesh," I say chuckling.

Io exhales and I feel the tension in her slight frame melt away. I set her down so I can get a good look at her. She appears unharmed. She smiles up at me with shinning tears in her warm brown eyes. I tuck a strand of hair behind her left ear. She closes her eyes as my hand brushes against her face. I feel the heat rising from her rosy cheek.

"We need to get back to the lake," Io says gravely. "Time is running out."

"Let's go," I say taking her hand.

"I need to find Kellan," Terra says firmly.

I blink, I completely forgot that Io and I were not alone in the room. Io turns to Terra. "We'll find him."

I frown at the exchange. The last time I laid eyes on these two they were hell bent on killing each other. *We'll broach that subject some other time.*

"Where could he be?" I ask.

"As I said when you first arrived," the High Priestess says in an exasperated tone. "Kellan is not here."

"Great. Let's get going," I say brightly.

Terra shoots me an angry glare. "I am not leaving without speaking to him."

"Suit yourself. Io and I are getting out of

here. We need to get back before sunrise. Remember?"

"Go on without me," Terra says. "I'll find him myself."

"Maybe it is for the best," Io says gently.

"You two go on. I'll catch up," Terra says firmly.

Io pulls Terra to her chest. Terra stiffens at the unexpected gesture. She gingerly pats Io's back.

"Hurry," Io says. Terra nods and gives Io a smile that does not reach her icy blue eyes.

Io turns away and Terra's brave facade slips. I see fear and despair in her eyes. Terra meets my gaze. "Get her back to the lake. I'll see you on the other side."

I nod as I take Io's hand in mine. The High Priestess presses a small package into Io's hand. Io gives her a hug. The High Priestess whispers something in Io's ear. Io smiles and nods.

"Thank you, Wren," I say offering my hand.

Wren clasps it and gives me a small smile. "Safe travels."

"Thank you for bringing us together," Io says to Wren.

"My pleasure," Wren says giving Io a hug.

Io and I step into the night. "I thought I'd lost you," Io says.

"You can't get rid of me that easily," I tease.

"Let's get out of here. I have had enough adventures for a while," Io says.

I pull her into my arms and breathe in her scent, wildflowers and sage. Io rests her head against my chest. She steps back and tilts her head in the direction of the village. She takes off running and I laugh as I run after her.

CHAPTER 22

IO

I can't keep my eyes off of him, I keep studying the lines of his face, trying to memorize every detail. Rowan and I begin the long climb to the top of the ridge. I keep squeezing his hand to make sure he is real. He traces small circles with his thumb on the back of my hand. I am comforted by his warm touch, it feels like liquid fire spreading through my veins. I devour the ground with long strides, eager to get as far from this place as possible. We ascend in a comfortable silence. I put one foot in front of the other, each step brings us closer to home.

We reach the top and I look back down on the Valley of Bones. *Get out of there, Terra.* I hope that she will not linger. Strange to think that a few weeks ago I was ready to strangle her. *She has grown on me.* It seems our adventure through the Underworld has sparked an unlikely friendship.

Rowan illuminates our shadowy surrounding with his brilliant blue flames. He grips his sword in his opposite hand. I keep mine at the ready. A sudden snap of a twig to my left launches me into the air in a panic. Rowan swings to the left, holding his flame engulfed hand high. A pair of large yellow eyes peers at us from the shadows. The eyes draw closer to the light and our monster takes shape, a *Direwolf.* I have only heard bedtime stories about these mysterious creatures. Three times the size of a normal wolf, with the strength and agility to best any predator. He is gorgeous, deep grey fur run through with white and black, larger than life paws, and gleaming white teeth. A growl rumbles from his throat as he stares us down.

I did not come this far to fail. Taking leave of my senses, I charge at the massive beast, screaming like a mad woman.

"IO!"

"Get out of here! Get back to the lake!"

The wolf crouches low and leaps forward, easily knocking me flat on my back and pinning me to the ground with a paw. I am plunged into darkness for a moment, my head spinning. My body goes limp.

A vague whizzing sound registers. I should run to safety but, I cannot get my muscles to respond. Everything hurts, I cannot remember what is going on. *Where am I?* A sudden blood chilling howl booms in my ears and my eyes snap open. I gaze up at the direwolf in horror. The wolf is desperately trying to gnaw an arrow shaft sticking out of his left shoulder. The pressure from his paw lets up slightly. I squirm and wriggle free. I spring to my feet and run. Thankfully the dire wolf's full attention is on the arrow. Two more arrows strike the wolf, he snarls and whimpers, his beautiful fur stained crimson.

I am mere paces from Rowan when I am slammed to the ground. I cry out as the wolf's claws rip the back of my dress.

"IO!"

"RUN!" I scream, struggling to reach my sword which is pinned beneath my right hip, the hilt digs into my upper thigh. Panic sets in. I start to hyperventilate, I scream in frustration. I feel hot, uncomfortably hot, the skin on my bare forearms starts to blacken. *Not again. This might be the only way to kill this vile beast.*

I stop struggling. I breathe as deeply as I can with the direwolf pressing me into the forest floor. *Focus. You ARE a Dragon! Unleash the fire.* My skin burns away to reveal sleek, shimmering obsidian scales, my fingers transform into curved claws. My wings sprout from my back, throwing the direwolf backward in a snarling heap. I spin around to face him. The direwolf tucks his tail between his legs as he cowers before me. I roar with all my might, "RAAAAAAAAAAWWWWWWWR-RRRRRRRRR!" The forest trembles around me. The direwolf turns and bolts into the forest's safe embrace. I raise my head and unleash a stream of fire to the night sky. My flames fly upward to lick the moon and incinerate the stars. I flap my wings, a great gust of wind violently shakes the trees, sending leaves swirling in a green flurry.

I bring my front legs down with a tremulous, earth rattling thud. I slowly turn to face Rowan. He is staring at me in wonder.

"You're a *Shapeshifter*. You are *Extraordinary.*"

I lower my head to Rowan's eye level. He gently strokes my face. I close my eyes at his touch. I feel myself shrinking, scales disappearing, replaced by warm tan skin, smooth hands, two legs, no more wings or thrashing tail, no more gleaming white fangs, or glowing golden fiery eyes. I suddenly feel faint. My knees buckle and Rowan catches me as I fall.

"I've got you. It's ok, you saved us, Io."

"Let's go home," I murmur as the world goes dark.

When I wake it takes a moment for me to remember. *The Realm of Lost Souls. Rowan!* I jerk violently, senses on high alert. Strong arms hold me with a vice like grip.

"Easy! It's alright. It's just me."

I still when I hear Rowan's voice. He sets me down on a large boulder. We are at the edge of the forest. The sky has lightened to a soft violet. *Time is almost spent. Dawn approaches.* I spring to my feet and nearly fall flat on my face.

"Take it slow," Rowan says steadying me.

"Let's get out of here. Dawn is coming."

Rowan takes me by the hand, we run for the double doors. We burst into the chamber off of Hekate's garden. Not a soul in sight. We leap across the stepping stones. We are out the front door and down the steep staircase in a heartbeat. I follow Rowan through the alleys and across the deserted village square. We make it back to the gates, the night guards see us approaching. They pull the heavy chains to open the enormous gate. The gap is just wide enough for us to dash through when we reach the doors. We keep running along the dirt road. I breathe in and out, pushing my legs faster and faster. My muscles burn from the effort, my heart races as we careen down the road kicking red dirt up in great clouds. Rowan slows his pace slightly so that I can catch up.

My heart leaps into my throat when I spot the hill top and the tree with the red blooms. Rowan gives my hand a gentle squeeze, flashing me a crooked smile. We race to the top of the hill. The surface of the lake is as smooth as glass. We wade in until we are standing waist deep in the black inky water. Rowan looks to me and I nod. We slip beneath the surface and swim down into the cold depths. I part the water with my outstretched hands, sweeping my arms back in long fluid strokes. I see a bright blue light glinting in the murky water. Rowan reaches a tentative hand toward the light, his hand slips through and disappears up to the wrist. When he pulls his arm back, his hand reappears. We clasp hands as we swim into the light.

"Io? Can you hear me?"

Rowan's voice sounds far off, like I am at the opposite end of a corridor hearing his faint call. I slowly open my eyes, the bright early morning light makes me squint. The room slowly comes into focus. I gaze up at the stained glass window with the black dragon, the sunlight filtering through the glass makes the dragon's eyes gleam gold. As I slowly come back to, my body makes me aware of every ache and pain. I groan as I try to sit up. Rowan helps me into a sitting position. I squeeze my eyes shut as the room tilts. I rest my head against Rowan's chest.

"I can hear you," I mumble.

Rowan laughs and kisses my forehead

softly. Rowan rises and offers me his hand, I place my hand in his and he pulls me to my feet. I walk into his arms. *When he holds me like this, I feel like I am home.* We slowly sway, side to side, taking in the moment.

"I thought I'd lost you," Rowan whispers in my ear.

"You can't get rid of me that easily," I whisper back.

Rowan tips my chin up. I stare into his gold flecked hazel eyes. His eyes move to my lips. I press up onto my tip toes and he brings his mouth to mine. *He is divine.* I lose myself in him. Everything else fades away. *There is only Rowan.*

CHAPTER 23

TERRA

"Where did he go when you sent him away?"

"He went to the west," the High Priestess says, pointing to the plains beyond the village."

"What is out there?"

"There are some gypsy tribes. They come to our valley to trade."

"Thank you, for your help," I say, turning to leave.

"Why not spare yourself the pain, child? He can never be the man you want him to be."

"I just need to say good bye," I say, unable to meet her eyes.

"Best get to it then. Your time is nearly spent. Make haste or you will spend eternity here."

I step out into the cool night air. I close my eyes and breathe, in and out. My heart slows to an even rhythm. I look to the trail leading to the ridge. Io and Rowan have surely reached the top by now. *I should have gone with them. What the hell am I doing? Risking my life for closure?*

As I walk I try to think of what to say to Kellan. *I miss you. I love you. I hate you.* I huff and puff as I power my way across the plains, sweat runs down my back. I wipe my forehead on my sleeve. I look back to the village. The bonfires blaze like beacons in the black of night. I can hear the drums. *It does not seem like a bad place to spend eternity.*

The plains are pitch black. I close my eyes and speak a simple spell, "*Solara.*" My upturned palm produces a bright white ball of light, it hovers and swirls just above my hand. I listen hard for any sounds that might alert me to hidden dangers. My heart hammers in my chest as I walk in through the darkness. I hear rushing water in the distance. *Great, the last thing I need is to get swept down a river.*

"I wouldn't go any further if I were you. Unless you're in the mood for a midnight swim."

I scream and jump back at the sound of his voice. Kellan steps into the light with a smirk on his face. I stand on shaking legs.

"How long have you been following me!?"

"For a ways. Just waiting for the right moment to announce myself."

"I think I just died a second time."

"What are you doing here, Terra?"

"I-I came to say goodbye"

"Quite an arduous trip for the sake of a farewell."

"Maybe I did not intend to return."

"We were not the right fit in life, Terra.

Death will not change that," Kellan says as he caresses my cheek.

I close my eyes and lean into his hand, tears running down my dirty cheeks. "We can start over."

"It is not your time," Kellan says with a sad smile. "Life is not done with you, Terra."

"There is nothing for me there," I sob. "I can't leave you here. Come with me."

"There is a whole world waiting for you. I am at peace here. I can be a better person, start fresh."

"You're MY person. I need you!"

"I will be with you always," Kellan says, pulling me to his chest.

I dissolve into a state of hysteria. We sink to the grassy ground and he rocks me like a small child until I cry myself out. I grip the front of his shirt, clinging to the person I despise and love with all my soul. Kellan kisses my forehead. He lays back and I snuggle into the crook of his arm. We lie together listening to the sounds of the night, the rustling of the breeze through the grass, crickets chirping, a wolf howling in the distance. I want to freeze this moment and live in it forever.

"It's time, Terra."

"Kiss me."

I tip my chin up to gaze into his eyes. He smiles down at me as he rolls me onto my back and kisses me with reckless abandon. I run my fingers through his hair as I press my hips up to his. We tear at our clothing, carelessly tossing them in all directions. A shiver dances down my spine as I feel the heat of his skin. I had no idea how much I needed this. Our breaths intermingle as he positions himself and thrusts inside me. I moan as we move together. Kellan looks down at me with tender eyes.

"I love you, Terra."

"I love you more."

"Says the woman who watched me die."

"Love is complicated."

Kellan laughs and shakes his head, "So it is."

"I came here to make it right."

"I am on board with your plan so far," Kellan says with a mischievous grin.

I nip his bottom lip and he rests his forehead against mine. We breathe each other in, one last time. Tears shimmer in my eyes, I blink them away. Kellan kisses me. I deepen the kiss, pulling him down to me. I run my hands down his bare muscular back. He moans against my lips, I smile. I let the tears fall as we break open and heal with every whispered sweet nothing and tender caress.

Kellan drapes his cloak around my shoulders, I wrap myself in it, breathing in his scent of pine trees and a mountain spring. Kellan collects our discarded clothing. He shakes the grass from my clothes before offering them to me. We dress in a comfortable silence. I turn to Kellan and he holds his arms out to me. I throw myself into his embrace, he holds me close, I can feel the steady beat of his heart. I grip him so tightly that my arm muscles strain from the effort. He does not try to pull away. I have no idea how long we stand this way. I take a deep breath before I look up at him.

Kellan smiles down at me. He kisses me, running one hand through my hair as the other holds my waist. When we come up for air I see tears in his eyes.

"I'll see you again, down the road."

The tears flow once more, "I won't keep you waiting long."

"I will always love you, Terra. I will spend eternity proving it."

"I love you, Kellan."

Kellan lets go and I turn away. The first few steps are the hardest. I look back and he is gone. I run back toward the Valley of Bones, angrily swiping my tear stained face with the back of my hand. I run hard, desperate to out run the gaping wound in my chest. The empty hollow feeling in my soul. I slow as I approach the edge of the village. The bonfires have burned down to glowing embers. The village is quiet. I weave my way through the empty streets. When I reach the foot of the trail, I have calmed down considerably. I begin my climb. *Just keep putting one foot in front of the other. You can do this.*

I stop at the top of the ridge to catch my breath. I look past the village to the dark plains. A sudden flickering of golden light catches my eye. Thousands of fireflies are rising from the grasslands, in shimmering golden clouds. *You know how much I love fireflies. Until we meet again, my love.* I summon my light and walk into the dark forest.

CHAPTER 24

ROWAN

I walk Io to her chambers so she can rest. I wait by the hearth while the maid helps her out of her dress behind a dressing screen. A platter of fruit, chicken sandwiches, and a pitcher of warm spiced cider has been laid out on the table before the hearth. I pop a grape into my mouth as I watch the flickering flames.

"You're frowning," Io says when she comes to stand next to me. "What's on your mind?"

"Just a strange feeling," I say. "It just feels like something is not right."

"Has anyone seen Terra yet?"

"No one has been able to find her. I am not sure if she made it back."

"Where would she have gone after she spoke with you?"

"Her Father's tower was burned to the ground. They had an old family cottage near the cliffs. We can check there."

Io and I walk down the corridor. We pass through the kitchens and slip out to the garden. A guard at the garden gate nods as we exit. Out of the castle walls, Io relaxes. I take her hand in mine. We follow the path to the sea cliffs. Nestled in a grove of lemon trees is a stone cottage with a red tile roof. A tendril of smoke is rising from the chimney. I knock on the red door. I try the knob and the door gives way. We step inside. I keep my hand on my sword hilt. The entry way is neat and tidy, the stone floor has been swept, a side table holds a large vase of freshly cut flowers. Two pairs of worn leather boots next to the door.

Up ahead on the left there is a kitchen with a large stone wash basin, a hearth, stone fire oven, and a walk in pantry stocked with provisions. A large pot is simmering over the fire. It smells like carrot ginger soup. A long wooden table is laid out with steaming fresh baked bread, apples, pomegranates, and assorted berries. A small platter of cheeses and nuts sits next to a large pitcher of lemon water.

"I knew you two would make it."

I turn to see Terra leaning against the door frame, she is a little worse for wear but, otherwise unharmed. Io gives her a small smile. She smiles back. I can see the flicker of pain in her eyes.

"Sit. I'll make some tea."

Io and I take a seat at the table. I have no appetite. I can barely keep my eyes open. I rub Io's back. She leans against me, softening at my touch. I kiss the top of her head. I feel a stab of guilt when Terra averts her eyes. Io sits up straight to create some distance between us.

"Are you alright?" Io asks, brows creased with concern.

Terra opens her mouth but, hesitates. She simply nods. Io lets the matter drop. Terra places a powder blue tea pot painted with white roses in the center of the table. She sets out three tea cups and saucers. Io pours the tea. I add a heaping spoonful of honey to my tea. Io does the same. Terra runs her finger along the rim of her tea cup. Her eyes are red, her eyelids swollen. Io reaches out and grasps Terra's hand. Terra looks up from her tea cup, eyes brimming with tears. Io stands up and walks over to give her a hug. Io wraps her arms around Terra as she sobs silently, tear drops falling into her tea cup.

Terra cries herself to sleep. I carry her to bed. Io pulls off her boots and tucks her in. Io smooths the hair from her face and kisses her forehead. "Rest now," Io whispers.

"Feeling up for a walk?" I ask.

"Sure, we can come back and check on her."

I lead Io to a narrow trail that runs down to the sea shore. We walk along the beach. I watch the crashing waves draw the sand out to sea, taking our foot prints with it. I see the break in the rocks up ahead, the cave mouth.

"I used to play here as a kid. We'd collect shells for our Mothers. Have stick sword fights."

We wander into the cave. The walls and floor have been worn smooth by the waves. I sit down on a large boulder while Io runs her hand along the stone wall. Io walks back to me. I stand to offer her my seat. Io reaches for my hand instead. I pull her closer. My heart flutters at her proximity. I place my hands on her waist. Io presses her hips into mine. I gaze at her with smoldering desire. Warmth floods my body.

I loosen the laces of her bodice, slipping a hand beneath her shirt. Io freezes, suddenly pale and panicked.

"Io? We don't have to do this," I say pulling away.

"I want to." Io insists. "I am taking my power back. This is my life. I am going to live it," She says, stepping forward.

Io lifts the hem of my shirt over my head. She runs her hands down my broad chest to the flat plane of my stomach. I rest my hands on her hips. Io undoes my sword belt, slowly lowering it to the ground. I unlace my trousers, sliding them down slowly. I kick off my boots. Io gazes at my naked form.

"You're beautiful," She murmurs.

"Your turn," I tease.

Io pulls her shirt over her head and kicks her boots off before slipping out of her breeches. I drink her in, gently caressing every curve, trailing kisses down her neck and across her bare chest. I move down to her belly, kissing and tasting. I caress her rear as I lower my head to the apex of her luscious thighs and kiss her deeply. Io moans softly as she works her fingers through my hair. I spread my cloak out, slowly lowering Io down to the floor.

"Are you sure?"

Io nods. I position myself between her legs and ease into her. Io closes her eyes and arches her back, her breath rushes out of her. I am floating among the stars, an endless black oblivion dotted with glowing embers. We lose ourselves in each other. I drift through this euphoria, riding waves of pleasure as it builds and builds, finally over flowing in sweet release. I feel my fire surging to the surface. Blue flames dance along my skin. Instinctively, I pull away to protect Io from my fire. I am surprised to see golden flames emanating from Io. She turns her hands over, examining her fire. *A Shapeshifter and a Fire Elemental. A rare beauty, my Princess.* Our flames blend together, tendrils of gold and blue flames illuminate our cave sanctuary, casting our shadows against the stone walls. We lie tangled up for an eternity. Io rests her head on my chest and I run my hands up and down her bare back. Her raven hair cascades down her shoulders. Our contented, rhythmic breathing is a balm for my soul. We trace our fingers over bare skin, kiss, and whisper to each other.

CHAPTER 25

IO

We dress and head back up the cliff trail to Terra's cottage. My heart sinks when I see the door has been left ajar. Rowan draws his sword and rushes to the cottage. I draw my dagger as I make my way around the back. The back door has been thrown open, a smashed clay pot lies in ruins on the stone steps. Soil and uprooted daisies are scattered all around. A sharp pain blooms at the back of my skull, my knees buckle and I fall forward, tumbling through the open back door. My vision blurs and I struggle to rise.

"No need to get up on my account."

I know that voice. I manage to flip onto my back so I can get a look at my attacker. That must have been a serious blow. *I don't believe my eyes. Is that? Mara?*

"Surprise. I've missed you, Io. You've been a busy bee. Making new friends. Losing your maidenhead. My, my. We must catch up."

"Mara? How?"

"Well dear sister, after you left me for dead, King Eamon's men found me. They took me back to the castle and fixed me up."

"What are you doing here?" I ask as my vision slips in and out of focus. My eyes start to droop.

"Coming to avenge my homeland, of course," Mara seethes.

Mara kneels down, placing her face close to mine, her eyes burn with malice. "I am going to burn your world to the ground. Come now, Io. There is much to be done."

Mara snaps her fingers. Two Elarian soldiers appear. One brute scoops me into his arms and carries me out the back door. *Rowan!* I squirm feebly but, my head throbs painfully. My eyes slide shut as I slip into the darkness. The last thing I see is a brown mare as I am slung over the saddle like a sack of grain. *Rowan, find me.*

I smell smoke and roasting meat. I can feel rough rope tightly binding my wrists behind my back. I peer through my eye lashes, I am lying on my side. In front of me sits a fallen log covered in moss and fungi. A fire burns bright, I can hear several men talking jovially, sloshing ale from tankards as they drink by the fire.

"What does she want with the girl, anyway?"

"Dunno, don't care."

"She is quite succulent."

"Keep your hands off! Princess's orders."

"Relax, Ed. I won't touch your precious maiden."

I doze off and on as these buffoons yap. The last one finally stumbles to his tent. I press my wrists apart and grope around for a stone. I find a decent size rock and get to work. I rub the stone against the rope. I finally feel a few fibers snap, a wild hope blooms in my chest. I drag the rock back and forth. I cut through the last fibers and my bindings loosen considerably. I shake the ropes off, rubbing my raw, bleeding wrists. I peek over the log. Several tents are set up on the other side of the fire. I lay still for a moment, listening hard. There might be someone patrolling the perimeter. I will have to move stealthily to get away undetected.

I crawl on my belly to a large oak tree. I peer into the darkness. There is not a soul in sight. I rise to a crouch and dart to the next tree. I hide behind the trunk, scanning for any sign of life. I dash from tree to tree until I can no longer see the camp fire. I walk silently through the woods, when I reach the edge of the forest the sky has lightened to lavender. I run the rest of the way back to the Black Keep. The guards on the castle walls open the gates when they see me approaching. I burst into the great hall where Rowan and my Grandfather are arguing heatedly with a group of warriors. Every head turns in my direction. I pluck a leaf from my disheveled hair and dust dirt from the front of my crumpled shirt.

Rowan's face floods with relief when he sees me. I give him a small smile. When he reaches me he frowns at the dried blood in my hair, my raw wrists.

"What happened?"

"It was Mara. Did you find Terra? Mara was at the cottage. She tried to bludgeon me to death."

"Well thank the stars she is inexperienced."

I laugh and Rowan pulls me in for a rib cracking hug. *Home at last.*

"Terra is fine. I can't say the same for the Elarian who tried to take her."

"Mara is coming for us. She intends to destroy Caelen."

"We'll be ready for her."

"I may have a few tricks up my sleeve," I say.

Rowan smiles, pressing a kiss to my forehead. I sink into his arms. Rowan guides me back to my chambers. A roaring fire burns in the hearth. The tub has been filled with steaming water. I peel off my filthy clothes and step into the tub. I undo my braids and rinse the grit from my hair. I scrub the grime from my skin with a wash cloth and rosemary peppermint soap. The bath water is a dull grey when I stand. Rowan offers me a towel. I dry my body and squeeze the excess water from my dripping hair.

I pull on a simple sky blue cotton shift dress. I sit down in an armchair by the fire. Rowan pulls a comb through my wet hair. I close my eyes as he braids with deft fingers. I stand and kiss him. Rowan holds me close, gripping my hips. I pull away and he lifts my into his arms. He carries me to the bed and tucks me in.

"Time for bed."

"I'm not tired," I say with a frown.

"You are a terrible liar," Rowan says dismissing my protest.

"Stay with me?"

"There is no where else I'd rather be," Rowan says. He lies down next to me.

I lay my head on his chest, listening to the steady beat of his heart. *The sweetest lullaby.* I close my eyes. Rowan rubs my back and kisses the top of my head. I fall into a deep sleep. Then the dreams begin.

I am standing in a field, the world is burning. Thick black smoke rises, blotting out the sky, making my eyes water and my lungs burn. Flames higher than my head rage all around me. I spin around trying to find a clear path. I see a dark silhouette through the smoke. A woman steps through the smoke, the Goddess Hekate.

"Hello, Io."

"Am I dead?"

"Far from it, dear heart. I bring a message."

"A message?"

"A warning. Princess Mara has gathered many allies to fight for her cause. She is coming to destroy all you hold dear. Her victory would mean the end of our world. She seeks to destroy all magic."

"Great, no pressure at all," I mutter.

"Do not despair, my child. Everything you need is within."

The Goddess fades back into the smoke. A crack of thunder overhead tips my face skyward, the rain falls in icy sheets, soaking me to the bone. The flames are extinguished. The blackened earth steams as the raindrops soothe the scorched soil. The ground is a swamp of mud and ash. I look down into a black puddle, a scaly black face and smoldering, fiery eyes stare back at me. I touch my face in alarm but, it is smooth and human.

I open my eyes, Rowan's sleeping face is the first thing I see. I run a finger down the right side of his face. He sighs sleepily.

"Good Morning," he murmurs.

"Good Morning," I say, stifling a yawn.

Rowan pulls me to his chest. I revel in his warm embrace. *Let them come. Together we are a force to be reckoned with, together we will burn this old world to the ground.*

ACKNOWLEDGMENTS

Mahalo to my amazing Ohana, your love and support mean everything to me. To my husband, Taj, thank you for being my best friend and a loving father to our tribe, there is no one else I would rather do life with.

I would like to thank Deffi Lesmawan for the exquisite cover design. Your artwork is stunning. I am honored to have it as a part of my story.

To my friend and incredible Book Coach,

Laura Reid, thank you for walking this path with me! Your support and guidance through the writing and publishing process has been wonderful. Cheers to future books and adventures! 💧🐉🔥

ABOUT THE AUTHOR

Amy Elizabeth Johnson was born and raised in Hawai'i, where the lush wilds of the islands shaped her imagination and forged her strength. A former Army Combat Veteran and lifelong warrior at heart, Amy takes to the skies to channel her power in the air as a circus artist on her aerial silks.

When her feet are on the ground, she is a devoted wife, mother, fantasy fanatic, and creator of written magic. Amy lives on a farm surrounded by her beloved Ohana, an array of animals (including a cat, dogs, horses, sheep, chickens, and cows), and beautiful surroundings straight out of a fairy tale.

A lover of bold heroines, epic love stories,

and adventures that demand everything, Amy was born to write this book. Blood of the Dragon is her spellbinding debut- a fierce tale of courage and perseverance that proves, the quiet girls roar loudest.

instagram.com/wildflower.circus808

www.ingramcontent.com/pod-product-compliance
Lightning Source LLC
Chambersburg PA
CBHW020947310726
48980CB00001B/83

* 9 7 9 8 9 9 8 6 3 5 1 3 7 *